TO WOO A HIGHLAND WARRIOR

Heart of a Scot
Book Four

By
COLLETTE CAMERON®

Blue Rose Romance®

Sweet - to - Spicy Timeless Romance®

USA Today Bestselling Author
COLLETTE CAMERON
Sweet-to-Spicy Timeless Romance®

For permission requests, write to the publisher at the address below.

Attn: Permissions Coordinator

info@collettecameronbooks.com

collettecameronbooks.com

eBook ISBN: 978-1-954307-74-2

Print Book ISBN: 978-1-966087-38-0

FREE BOOK!

JOIN MY EXCLUSIVE MAILING LIST
Collette Cameron Newsletter

AND GET A FREE EBOOK!

https://collettecameronbooks.com/freegift

Plus Sneak Peeks, Giveaways, Contests, Exclusive Content, and More... P.S. I promise only good stuff ~ **no** spam!

*To Collette's Chèris—the most fantastical
author-reader group ever!
I love you!
xoxo*

ONE

Scottish Highlands
Early September 1720

A hair-raising scream rent the late afternoon's soggy air, wrenching Liam MacKay, Baron of Penderhaven, from his melancholy musings. He snorted in derision. When in these past five years weren't his reflections melancholic? Macabre even?

Astride Deri—so named for the gelding's metallic-shaded coat—he reflexively clasped the dirk at his waist as the pulverizing wind caught the merest wisp of another frantic cry. Pulling his spine straighter, all of his senses acutely alert, he squinted through the deluge pelting him and methodically scrutinized the surrounding woodlands.

From whence had the shout come?

Close by, for certain.

Eyes narrowed, he scratched his beard and made a thorough, circular study of the area once more. The tangy scent of sodden earth and the sharp, almost pungent, odor of the shrewish tempest met his flared nostrils.

With the furious squall buffeting the thrashing trees and the torrential rain hammering the drenched ground—not to mention the periodic deafening booms of thunder hard on the heels of each lightning streak illuminating the heavens—he couldn't quite discern the person's location or gender. Another incandescent purplish flash divided the bruise-colored sky, immediately followed by an earth-shaking explosion in the firmaments.

God's teeth, what a gale.

In his one and thirty years, he didn't recall a more sudden or violent thunderstorm. The ground was still hard and arid from an unusually warm summer, and water gushed down the craggy hillside, eager to reach the riotous brown river below.

More than once, Deri had slid on the slick slope. If there'd been lodgings to be had this past hour, Liam would've sought its refuge straightaway.

Traveling in this sorry weather was stupid, plain and simple. But halting and risking the elements might prove worse with the trees snapping like kindling all around Liam. Unrelenting stinging rain pellets lashed his face, giving no hint of reprieve anytime soon either.

For the past three hours, the powerful thunderstorm raging overhead had battered the Highlands. Which explained why he'd chosen to ride beneath the flailing branches above rather than chance the open road a few hundred yards away.

Quite simply, there was far less risk of lightning striking him amongst the trees than upon the unprotected track paralleling the river. However, in these woodlands, a much greater risk of being taken down by a falling tree existed.

Odin's teeth. Damned if he did and damned if he didn't. A no-win situation. Caught between the coals and the cookpot.

Head angled as he strained to hear above the storm, he pushed his saturated hair off his forehead. Another terrified shriek—*definitely feminine*—echoed through the Scots pine forest, curdling his blood and raising his nape hair, as well as causing his horse to sidestep and snort nervously.

"Easy, lad. Shh." He hugged his knees to the gelding's sides, giving him a reassuring pat on the neck. Whoever the woman was, he couldn't ignore her terrified cries. He stroked the horse again. "Dinna fash yerself, my friend."

"Unhand me, *vous monstre!*"

Monster and in French to boot?

"Help! Help! *Mon Dieu.* Somebody, help us, *s'il vous plait.*" The last broke on a ragged sob, barely audible above the thunder reverberating violently in the angry pewter sky.

What in Odin's toes was a French woman doing in this isolated stretch of the Highlands, in this godawful weather, and screaming for help? To be fair, the storm had developed quite suddenly, and the nearest inn was miles away.

Nonetheless, his warrior's instinct pinged an urgent warning.

And the Frenchwoman had said "us." Meaning more than one person was in some sort of danger. Hell, anyone outside in this hell-fired gale was in peril.

"*Mon Dieu, non. Non.*" The plaintive wail broke through a pause in the storm's tumult.

Desperate. Defeated. Disbelieving.

Swearing a steady stream of expletives beneath his breath, Liam reined Deri in the direction of the heart-rending plea and put his heels to the horse's sides. At once, the steed surged forward, pounding toward God only knew what. Liam erupted through the towering trees, momentarily taken aback at the bizarre scene before him.

A traveling coach angled across the middle of the mucky road, its door flung wide open. Two men, legs splayed and their bearing menacing, stood near the front of the vehicle. *The coachmen?*

A pair of dripping-wet women huddled together a few feet away, the taller with her arm wrapped protectively around the smaller woman's shoulders. Even from where he'd exited the woodlands, he couldn't miss the diminutive woman's violent quaking.

One driver gleefully brandished a pair of blunderbusses.

Christ on the cross.

What in the bloody hell went on here? A robbery? It didn't make sense. Why drive the ladies to this godforsaken spot? Especially in this rabid weather?

The fiend straightened his arm, aiming a weapon at the younger woman. "Say yer prayers, lass. 'Tis time to meet yer maker."

Not if Liam could help it.

Wrenching his dirk from his belt, he released a warrior's ferocious battle shout. Another peal of thunder split the turbulent shrapnel sky, muffling the bellow. He vaulted from the saddle. But before his feet hit the ground, the man, still grinning maniacally, pulled the trigger.

Nae!

"*Non!*" The skinny older woman threw herself in front of the other equally slender lady.

The taller female caught her companion in her arms, the

momentum from the gunshot propelling them to the muddy ground.

"Nae! Nae! *Naaee!* Aunt Jeneva!" the woman cried hoarsely, hunched over her immobile aunt, patting her face. "Och, my God, ye unconscionable monster. I think...ye've *killed* her."

Even as Liam surged across the remaining distance, the scunner's face contorted into a devious smirk, and he calmly leveled the other pistol at her head.

Proud and gloriously defiant, the lass lifted her chin, her saturated bronze tresses spilling over the plain dark blue cloak covering her shoulders and spine. Such bravery in the face of terrifying peril could only be admired, and Liam's warrior's heart applauded her courage.

An instant later, an uncomfortable jolt speared his breast.

He recognized her.

She'd been at the *cèilidh* hosted by Graeme Kennedy a few weeks ago. And also at that ludicrous masked ball in Edinburgh that Mother had insisted he escort his sister, Kendra, to.

"Why? Why are ye doin' this?" she shakily asked, her delicate, stricken face streaked with tears and rain. "We've nae money or jewels. Nothin' of value. We're simple seamstresses."

The wind whipping his hair, the coachman shrugged casually, as if they discussed the petulant weather. He hastily sliced his companion a sly side-eyed look. "We've been paid handsomely to dispose of ye."

Her mouth went slack, and a confused line appeared between her brows. "Ye must have the wrong person. I'm nae a threat to anyone. Neither was my aunt. We have nae enemies. Ye've made a horrendous mistake."

"Nae. 'Tis nae mistake." He grinned, exposing time-yellowed teeth and wobbled the gun's muzzle up and down. "We made absolutely sure of yer identity, Miss Emeline Toinette Jeneva LeClaire, didna we, Hamish?"

"Aye, that we did," his compatriot agreed, returning his friend's sneaky sidelong glance. "Such a fancy name. So lady-like. I still say we ought to sample the bonnie lass, Walter. Nae one will ever ken, and it seems such a waste no' to. How often do we get to sink our wicks into a lady? A pretty one too, even if she is a skinny rickle-a-bones lass."

Over Liam's dead body would they lay so much as a finger upon her.

Eyes rounding in comprehension, she blanched and cast a frantic glance to either side.

"Ye have a good point, my friend." Walter licked his fat lips, his lewd gaze lingering on the gentle swells the cloak hid. "A verra good point. He didna say we couldna, did he? He only said to make sure she didna return to Edinburgh alive."

Who, exactly, was the *he* they referred to?

This was no random robbery then. It was an assassination. Liam didn't have time to ponder why, however, for the scoundrels were intent on ravishing the remaining woman before disposing of her as ordered.

All at once, the rotter became aware of Liam bearing down upon him—looking no doubt like a wrathful, bearded demon straight from the bowels of hell. His features contorting in fear and fury, the attacker staggered backward a step and veered the gun's muzzle toward Liam.

"Ye'll meet *yer* maker today, ye devil's spawn," Liam vowed in a guttural growl.

At a full sprint, he threw the dirk. Satisfaction flooded him as the blade lodged to the hilt in the blackguard's throat, and a stream of crimson gushed forth.

His eyes wide and surprised, the blunderbusses tumbled from the bounder's hands. Clutching his neck and making weird gurgling noises, he folded to his knees, then ever-so-slowly slumped forward.

Slapping a hand over her mouth, Emeline LeClaire choked on a gasp and speedily averted her attention from the grisly scene.

Yanking an evil-looking knife from his boot, the other churl crouched into a defensive position. He brandished the knife with the ease of someone accustomed to handling a blade.

Precisely who were these miscreants?

Liam would vow playing the part of coachmen wasn't their typical employment. It didn't matter. They'd breathed their last today.

He whipped his tartan around his arm. Using the plaid as a shield, he lowered his shoulders and barreled into the smaller man, slamming him into the coach with a sickening crunch.

The driver shrieked in pain and terror as Liam caught his neck in the crook of his elbow and, with one violent twist, broke the would-be-murder and rapist's neck. He crumpled to the ground, his lifeless eyes glazing over. He'd not be attacking any more defenseless women.

Liam mightn't ever want to marry again, but he'd never mistreat a woman or stand by and watch another do so either. Breathing harsh and his heart yet hammering an erratic drum-beat behind his ribs, he retrieved his dirk, a gift from his da for his sixteenth birthday. After wiping the blade clean on one of the dead men's coat, he slipped the knife into his belt.

"Aunt Jeneva." Her voice and expression anguished, Miss LeClaire rocked her ashen-faced aunt in her arms. Scarlet stained the older woman's unmoving chest and Miss LeClaire's gloves. "I'm sorry, Aunt, so verra sorry," she choked around her inconsolable weeping. "Ye wouldna be here if I hadna insisted we visit Berget," she moaned, her voice breaking.

Hurrying to her side, Liam squatted and put two fingers to the limp woman's neck, checking for a pulse. *Dead.* Lips pressed tight, he scanned the area, ensuring nobody else skulked about. "Lass, is there anyone else with ye?"

She dragged her watery gaze upward, her thick-lashed, brandy-colored eyes glazed and out-of-focus pools. The sprinkling of cinnamon-colored freckles stood out starkly on her high cheekbones and impertinent turned-up nose. She blinked sluggishly before her attention slid to the men, and a violent shudder racked her.

Shifting slightly, he maneuvered to partially block her gruesome view. The wind caught his plaid and slapped it against his thigh. The ferocious storm yet seethed around them, but she appeared to have retreated into her own hellish world.

"Lass?" He touched his fingertips to one shoulder.

"Nae." She swallowed, shaking her head and then biting her plump lower lip. "Nae one." Her voice was as lifeless as the woman draped across her lap.

"I'm Liam MacKay," he said softly in the soothing tone he used to speak to an unbroken horse. No need to mention he was also a baron. "I saw ye at Graeme Kennedy's gatherin' in August." He hadn't spoken to her and in doing so now, he violated rule number one: *Stay clear of innocent lasses.*

Her expression utterly lost and devastated, she didn't respond.

He hadn't remembered her name until the dead man said it, but Liam did recall her costume at the ball. A rather hideous shepherdess ensemble, complete with a ridiculous bonnet and staff—not that anyone had introduced them.

In general, Liam shunned women.

To be precise, he avoided unwed, marriageable lasses like the plague or pox. Snared once already in that unholy trap, he'd no intention of ever falling into that viper's pit or finding himself in a compromising position again. Kendra and her progeny could bloody well inherit the feudal barony.

Familiar grief cramped his lungs, the ache blooming in his chest and stealing his breath.

Nae. No' now.

Except, damn his eyes, he'd also broken rule number two in the past five minutes: *Never, ever, be alone with an unmarried woman.* Widows didn't count, and he'd found them most accommodating over the years.

"Ye're Emeline?" He knew her name, but forcing her to focus on something besides her dead aunt cradled in her arms was paramount.

"Aye, Emeline LeClaire," came her monotone response. "I remember ye." Her wary doe-eyed gaze slashed to the strip of puckered flesh marring his right cheek. "I've wondered several times how ye came by yer scar."

Not exactly the stuff of conversations, especially between strangers.

Kristin's doing, the night she'd tried to kill him. But he wasn't about to reveal that to a woman and one he didn't know. Again, his chest constricted, and he fought the helplessness the dreaded memories stirred.

Lightning lashed across the gloomy sky. Several more jagged flashes followed in quick succession, accompanied by resounding, earth-shaking crashes. Could the thunderstorm possibly be growing worse? Just then, the rain turned to hail. The cherry-sized pellets pummeled them like miniature cannonballs. Thunder exploded, roll after furious forceful roll, across the sky.

God's bones.

A peculiar rumbling echoed in the distance. Glowering, Liam glanced upriver.

What was he to do with this woman? Or the three dead people, for that matter?

Undecided, he sighed, plowing a hand through his soaking hair. He could tie Deri to the rear of the vehicle and drive the coach himself. At least Miss LeClaire would be out of this damnable weather.

He'd leave the assassins here. But he wasn't keen on placing the dead aunt inside the coach with the lass or securing her corpse with the luggage either. Besides, the miry road would make for painfully slow travel. What was more, he had no desire to endure the beastly weather perched atop the conveyance and a potential target for a lightning bolt.

Eyes oddly vacant and shoulders slumped in misery and grief, Miss LeClaire shivered. Tears careened down her wan cheeks, but she made no sound. Her silent agony tore at his consternation. Kristin had been a screamer.

He scowled again, frustration beating an irritating staccato down his spine.

It would take hours to reach shelter by coach. At least two

hours on horseback too. However, Deri could make the hunting lodge—the only accommodations within twenty miles and wholly inaccessible by any sort of traveling vehicle. In fact, when stocking the lodge—more a small cabin than grandiose accommodations—he used pack horses to carry the supplies.

As he stood upright, Liam eyed the mucky road and then the rising river with a practiced eye.

So much for making it home by nightfall.

This thunderstorm made reaching Eytone Hall impossible. He released the team before returning to Emeline. It would be cruel to leave them harnessed in this weather. God only knew how long it would be before someone could return for them. Days mayhap.

At once, the pair dashed toward the haven the woods provided. Smart animals.

"I'm goin' to put yer aunt inside the coach," he gently told Miss LeClaire. "I'll send my men for her as soon as the wynds are passable again."

Uncertainty and a hint of fragility in her gaze, she searched his eyes. Even sopping wet and strain etched across her face, he couldn't help but notice her refined features. He was still a healthy young man in the prime of his life, after all.

High cheekbones, a dainty, slightly upturned nose, almost too full lips, and unusual treacle-colored eyes, much too big for her face, met his perusal. Fingers curled into the fabric of her gray and burgundy traveling gown, she gave a stiff, barely discernable nod before presenting her rather aristocratic profile.

He sighed in relief that she hadn't fought him on the

matter. He'd have moved her aunt, with or without her consent, but he'd wasn't keen to rile her temper.

Over four hellish years of marriage had provided him a lifetime's worth of shrewish female behavior. The result was he had minimal patience for petulance, histrionics, and, most especially, female wiles.

Emeline leaned down and kissed her aunt's forehead. "I'm so verra sorry," she whispered brokenly before signaling Liam with a slight flexing of her eyes that she was ready for him to take the dead woman.

"Ye have my deepest condolences for yer loss, lass." It was hard enough to lose a loved one but to witness their murder— "I'll keep ye safe until ye reach yer home."

Och, mon, shut yer damned wheesht. She's nae yer responsibility. Dinna make promises ye canna keep or that might lead to misunderstandin's of a romantic nature.

He booted his recriminations to the roiling river. He was simply helping an unfortunate lass in desperate circumstances. Nothing more. Common decency demanded he do so.

Once he'd wrapped the dead woman in her cloak and placed her in the vehicle, he dragged the coachmen beneath the conveyance. Someone might recognize them, and that could lead to the person who hired them to kill Miss LeClaire.

At least he knew their names. *Hamish and Walter. Two verra common Scots names.* Nevertheless, that proved very fortunate and might help a great deal.

It was too soon to ask her who had cause to wish her dead, but it was a conversation she'd have to have. Either with Liam or the authorities. Probably both. Except, she'd claimed she had no enemies. *None she kens about.*

He swiped his forearm across his brow, not that the

gesture brought any reprieve. As if he weren't bloody uncomfortable enough, a combination of sweat and rain ran in irritating rivulets down his forehead and temples. Into his eyes too. The salty sweat stung, further obscuring his visibility.

He strode to Miss LeClaire and, hands on his hips, regarded her forlorn form. She hadn't moved. Likely shock had set in. Just what he needed—an incapacitated female miles from the nearest town and anyone who might aid them.

Hells clanging bells. Now he was breaking rule number three: *Never offer assistance to an unwed female.*

A dark stain marred the ground before her, and, for the first time, he noticed the crimson smeared across her chest. Pray God, it was her aunt's and not hers. He knew next to nothing about tending wounds.

The earsplitting roaring grew louder. Alarm bludgeoned Liam as he finally comprehended what the unearthly rumble meant. *Shite!* Giving a shrill whistle, he summoned Deri. He grasped Emeline's arms, pulling her unceremoniously to her feet. Peering into her blank umber eyes, he gave her a sharp shake.

"Lass! Flash flood!"

Every ounce of color drained from her already wan face. She gasped, jerking her attention behind him to the river.

"*God* above," she choked out, her voice thin with terror.

Deri trotted to Liam and tossed his head.

Liam brusquely lifted her onto the destrier, legs astride, and grabbed the reins. "Scoot back," he yelled, leaping into the saddle. "Hold on tight." He kicked Deri hard. "Go, lad! Go!"

The horse needed no encouragement. Deri bolted up the incline as the wall of fulminating water tumbled down the riverbed, sucking anything unfortunate enough to be in its path into the brownish-black, undulating mass. Leaning low, Liam urged the straining horse upward, away from the frothing, churning, *deadly* tumult.

Not a hair's breadth between them, Miss LeClaire clung to him, her wet head pressed into his back, her hands fisted together at his middle. Violent shudders shook her as her breasts scuffed his spine. Her breathing came in harsh little pants in between what, he suspected, might be supplications to The Almighty. *Good.* They needed all the help they could muster, divine or otherwise.

What seemed like hours later—in reality, only a mere handful of minutes had crawled passed—the gelding at last crested the hill. His sides heaving, he snorted and jerked his head up and down.

"I ken, laddie. I ken. Ye did verra well." Liam ran a hand down the horse's lathered neck. The poor beast needed a reprieve from this devilish tempest too. "Ye saved our lives, ye did."

He relaxed a fraction as he dismounted, then turned to survey the heaving, unforgiving waters. Had they been even five minutes later, the flood would've caught them too.

Of the coach, there was no sign. Likely, the three corpses would never be found either. At least not in identifiable condition. He'd not voice that unpleasant truth, however. The knowledge might prove more than Miss LeClaire could bear in her fragile state.

"Are ye all right, lass?" He glanced over his shoulder.

As all right as any woman who found herself in this dreadful situation might be. Despite the seriousness, he couldn't help but admire her long, milky white legs, bared to just above the thigh.

He wasn't *dead*, for God's sake. Nor a monk. Just a man who deliberately steered clear of innocent maidens.

Face pale as death, she raised her head, that umber-tinted owlish gaze round and uncertain. Her pale pink lips parted. "I..." The next instant, her eyes rolled back into her head.

Arms outstretched and uttering an oath, Liam lurched toward his horse and caught her limp form.

TWO

Emeline gradually awoke, becoming aware she lay on her side atop an unyielding surface. A nagging sense that something was horribly wrong prodded her awake. Simultaneously, another part of her insisted she surrender to sleep's blessed forgetfulness once more.

Feeling as if bricks weighted her eyelids, she edged them open. God save her; the effort was almost too much.

Across the room from where she lay, a fire burned low in a soot-stained stone hearth. Its failing glow cast weird shadows upon the equally bucolic walls. Eyebrows pinched in confusion, she raised her gaze a fraction. A rough-hewn ceiling met her bleary inspection.

What was this place?

Where was this place?

The last thing she recalled was sitting astride a massive gray-toned horse amidst a fierce storm.

Or had she dreamed that?

Disoriented and her forehead furrowed, she skimmed her palm over the rough blanket covering her on the narrow bed built into the cottage's wall. A series of memories came crashing back, encapsulating her in a tidal wave of anguish.

A bearded tartan-clad Highlander chargin' across the road, dirk in hand.

A flash flood bearin' down upon us.

Clingin' to a broad, muscular back.

The two men wantin' to kill me.

Aunt Jeneva! Och, God. God. Aunt Jeneva is dead. Dead!

Eyes pooling with scorching tears, she gulped in a great rush of air. Fear and sorrow speared her, eviscerating her with pain equal to being cleaved in half. She jerked upright, cracking the top of her head on another shelf-like bed directly above hers.

Ouch!

Soft snores echoed nearby and, blinking away her tears while rubbing her sore head, she stared hard at the wooden slats mere inches from her face.

Was *he* up there?

The man with the ridiculously muscled back and chest? And the wild, untamed silver-streaked mane of raven hair and equally wild beard? The brave Scot who'd risked his life to save her?

What was his name?

She put two fingers between her eyes and gently pressed.

Liam. Liam MacKay.

And according to her dear friend, Berget Jonston, not just a Scot but the Baron of Penderhaven. Although, truth to tell, the fierce man who rescued her resembled an uncivilized warrior rather than a feudal baron and laird of an extensive estate.

She licked parched lips.

God, she was thirsty.

Holding her breath, she flung back the blankets. She swung her legs over the edge of the cot and paused for a moment, waiting for the sickening dizziness causing her head to spin like a child's toy top to subside. After she inhaled a few deep breaths, the swirling ceased, and she further examined the humble cottage's interior in the muted light.

It might well be a rustic hunting lodge. No, lodge was far too generous a description. Cramped cabin better described the simple rectangular, single-room building. Everything about its interior heralded masculinity, from the barren walls to the crude, no-nonsense furnishings. The adjacent wall boasted another pair of bunks.

Ah, there in the lower bunk, his immense size dwarfing the small area, slumbered her savior.

One elbow slung across his face, he lay on his back. A gray-brown coarse woolen blanket like hers covered his torso. His sculpted chest, deliciously sprinkled with curly midnight hair, lay bare for Emeline's inspection.

She unashamedly looked her fill.

Indecently large muscular arms and a thickly corded neck gave testament to his strength. Strength she'd experienced first-hand. Earlier, he'd picked her up and plopped her atop his horse as if she weighed no more than a loaf of bread.

Though she wasn't one to ogle the opposite sex, Emeline would have to have been dead not to appreciate what a marvelous specimen of manhood Liam MacKay, Baron of Penderhaven, presented.

Seldom—*fine, never*—had she seen the like. If she hadn't been so traumatized by the series of events which had occurred but hours ago, she might've thrilled at the recollection of his touch and the generous amount of exposed virile masculinity before her now. If she were a woman who took note of such provocative displays.

She put her fingers to her ribs where she could still feel the imprint of his large palms spanning them. A flush of sudden mortification scoured her, and she flattened her hand on her torso. *Good heavens.* She wore nothing but her shift.

Where were her clothes?

Scrutinizing the cottage, Emeline relaxed slightly upon spying her gown, cloak, and stockings. They, along with Liam's garments, had been draped over a thin rope that stretched from one side of the room to the other. He'd placed her shoes and his knee-high boots on either side of the hearth.

At the realization he'd undressed her, another blush swept her from ankle to neck.

She'd fainted. Dead away.

Before today, she'd never swooned. However, she supposed, given the horrific events of the past few hours, a moment of womanly weakness was acceptable.

Satisfied she'd not have to parade about in the presence of a man in nothing but her underthings, she finished inspecting the lodgings.

A scruffy table with four mismatched chairs sat in the middle of the single-room abode. Beside the door, a six-paned window—the only one—looked out onto the inky sky. Glass was highly unusual for a humble abode such as this, shutters being much more common and less expensive.

The fireplace dominated the final wall. Next to it, a shelf contained all manner of items from books to cups and plates to what appeared to be a chess set. A motheaten, slightly crooked stag head hung directly above the fireplace. Pegs protruded from the posts bracing the beds and from the door as well.

Sparse. Plain. Functional. A man's abode, for certain.

The baron's?

Emeline swallowed against the dryness scraping her throat. *Water.* She must have a drink of water. When she was positive she could stand without falling onto her face, she braced one hand against the wall and gingerly levered to her feet.

The floor was freezing, and she almost jerked them back beneath the blanket.

"What the devil do ye think ye're doin', lass?"

Liam's husky, sleep-thickened question so disconcerted her, she gave a tiny yelp and jumped. She tottered unsteadily for an instant.

"Ye startled me," she said inanely. *Och, for pity's sake.* Shaking off her discomfit, she made a feeble gesture. "I'm thirsty. Is there any water to be had?"

That was the God's honest truth. Her mouth felt as dry as parchment.

Half-groaning and half-sighing, he sat up. Although, unlike her, he was careful not to smack his head on the upper bunk. The blanket slid to his waist, revealing even more of his gorgeous body, including the rippled muscles of his sinewy torso and the stair-steps of his ribs.

As irrational as it was, she envied the blanket. For it was permitted to caress that fascinating flesh while she was not.

Attention fixed on him, she worked her captivated gaze over every inch of exposed flesh. How very different a man's body was from a woman's.

Emeline swallowed again and dropped her attention to the floor, suddenly finding her cold, pink toes quite the most enthralling things. Not as enthralling as the man in yonder bed, however.

Was he totally nude beneath the blanket?

At once, all sorts of naughty—delicious—images leaped to mind.

God help her and her vivid imagination. She wasn't convinced the peculiar flutterings in her stomach were dismay at all. She studiously kept her focus fixed on the worn floor as he rustled around a bit.

"Ye can look now, lass." Distinct humor colored his rumbling burr.

Expecting to see him clothed, she glanced up. Her jaw sagged like a worn-out cushion, and the tingles shooting through her had nothing to do with disapproval or censure. *Good God*. Flames licked her already hot cheeks.

He'd simply secured the blanket haphazardly around his narrow waist.

Had the man no sense of decency?

No, that wasn't at all fair.

Hadn't he risked his life to rescue her but hours ago?

She was made of sterner stuff than to get her feathers ruffled over a man's naked chest. And deliciously carved torso. And the tantalizing strip of coal-black hair disappearing into the blanket...

Even if he was spectacular enough to rival Hercules. Adonis. Apollo. Zeus.

My word, she'd been so cold but a few moments ago. However, such was certainly not the case now. No indeed. Her swallow this time was more of a gulp of overpowering, sensual awareness.

Dragging her musings from dangerous paths, she forced

logic and reason to the forefront of her mind. Undoubtedly, Liam's clothing had been as saturated as hers. To expect him to sleep in the sodden garments to preserve her sensibilities—especially when she'd been insensate—was preposterous.

He motioned to a pail atop a narrow table beneath the window. "There's fresh water in the bucket." His long strides eating up the short distance, and his bare feet making soft slapping noises, he strode across the room. Dark sable hair covered his calves and even sprinkled his toes.

Never before had she considered a man's feet sexy. But when had she ever seen a man's feet before? *Good God.* She didn't have a warped foot fetish, did she?

He filled the cup, then lifted it toward her. "Come, doe eyes. Dinna be shy."

Doe eyes?

She rather liked that.

Conscious of the thin fabric covering her, Emeline seized a blanket off her bunk and, after wrapping it around her shoulders, crossed to him. She greedily drank the soothing water. The cool, sweet liquid was balm to her aching throat. Crying always made her throat hurt.

Anguish assailed her again, and she thrust the cup at him as she aimed her gaze to the floor.

Aunt Jeneva was dead. *Dead.*

Strict, a devout woman of faith, and disposed to punitiveness, she hadn't been the kindest or most nurturing person. But she was the only mother Emeline had ever known. Her own had died giving birth to her. And now, she had no one, other than distant second or third cousins in France that she'd never met and had no desire to.

My God. What was she to do?

The position of governess for Laird Graeme Kennedy's nieces was available. Emeline wanted to accept the offer of the position. However, Aunt Jeneva, in her typical formidable manner, had forbidden it.

Nonetheless, at four and twenty, Emeline had reached the end of her patience and tolerance with her aunt's demands and restrictions. She'd told her friend Berget Jonston that after returning to Edinburgh, she intended to have a very candid conversation with Aunt Jeneva, and then she would strike out on her own.

Fate had deemed that wasn't necessary now. No, not fate. A pair of despicable bounders.

Nonetheless, she wasn't exactly destitute. Besides the governess post, there was Aunt Jeneva's modestly successful and very exclusive modiste shop in Edinburgh.

Truth to tell, though, Emeline wasn't altogether as keen on sewing for a living as her aunt had been. The craft had been a way to earn a living and never a great passion. Employment as a governess didn't exactly thrill her either but at least she'd have been out from beneath her aunt's reproachful eye.

That troublesomeness no longer existed. For the first time in her life, she was free to do what she wanted. That freedom had come at a tremendous cost, however.

Emeline could sell the modiste business, she supposed. She assumed she'd inherit the shop, albeit, Aunt Jeneva hadn't discussed anything of that nature with her.

To think she'd never see her aunt's lace-capped head bent over her current commissioned garment, steadily stitching away, brought another wave of grief. A ragged sob escaped her, and she slapped a palm over her mouth, swiftly spinning away from Liam.

"Och, lass, come here."

Resignation, reluctance, and compassion tinged his roughed voice. He came up behind Emeline and gently turned her toward him, engulfing her in the warm circle of his arms. Smoothing the fly-away hair from her face with one huge hand, he lightly caressed between her shoulder blades with the other. "I ken ye've had a terrible shock. And I ken ye need time to accept what has happened. I'll nae abandon ye. Never fear."

More unexpected kindness from this gruff man who didn't owe her anything.

She didn't even pretend she didn't desire his comforting embrace. She snuggled deeper into the broad breadth of Liam's firm chest, welcoming this stranger's soothing touch, desperately needing what he so gallantly offered. His crisp chest hair tickled her nose, and she inhaled his manly scent. He smelled of horse and rain and something slightly spicy. Manly.

He smelled of temptation.

And even in her distress, something undefinable burgeoned deep within her.

If sorrow hadn't overwhelmed, she might've taken the time to appreciate the wonderfulness. As it was, however, she wept brokenheartedly for the aunt who'd sacrificed her life to protect her.

Up until today, Emeline had always felt an imposition thrust upon her mother's spinster sister and had doubted Aunt Jeneva cared for her. What an unbearable way to discover just how much her aunt had loved her, after all.

After several long moments of Liam murmuring soothing things in Gaelic into her hair while platonically skimming his palms over her shoulders and spine, she snuffled indelicately and stepped away.

Chagrined and self-conscious, she murmured, "Thank ye. Ye've been most kind, and I ken that I have inconvenienced ye greatly. I owe ye my life, and I am truly grateful to ye."

Sniffing again, she dabbed at her damp face with the scratchy blanket.

As if uncomfortable with her appreciation, he inclined his head minutely and clasped his nape with a hand. "I washed yer gown and cloak as best I could, but they're still stained." He looked pointedly at her chest covered by the plain blanket.

Mouth turned down, she lowered her gaze to her bosoms. She hadn't even noticed if her chemise bore evidence of her aunt's blood. Nausea swirled in her belly at the thought. "Thank ye."

What other man would've been so considerate? So chivalrous?

He lifted a flask from beside the bucket and removed the cap. After taking a healthy swig, he offered, "Whisky?"

"Nae, thank ye." On her empty stomach, she feared she'd become ill. She'd never sampled anything stronger than port before, and that only rarely.

He replaced the flask on the table, then rested his hip against the edge. Arms folded, emphasizing his bulging pectoral muscles—*how does a man acquire muscles that big?*— and seemingly totally at ease in his undressed state, he canted his head slightly. Expression solemn, his eyes the same shade as the petulant sky during the tempest, he regarded her.

She quelled the child-like urge to shuffle from one foot to the other.

"The storm finally ceased about two hours ago," he said. "But there are many downed trees and mudslides. And I'm sure other waterways are flooded as well. When the roads are unencumbered, my home is less than a quarter day's journey from here."

She scrunched her nose as she adjusted the blanket around her shoulders and shifted her feet, suppressing a shiver. She'd grown cold once more.

Had he mentioned where his home was? Had Berget?

"However, with Deri obliged to carry us both, and the likelihood we'll encounter hazardous roadways, I've nae doubt it will take us considerably longer." He cut a short, almost impatient glance out the window. "I dinna think we can safely leave here for at least a day, perhaps more. The ground is saturated and unstable."

Emeline made an inarticulate sound and touched her fingers to her throat as disappointment crested up her chest. She'd hoped—believed—they'd leave first thing in the morn.

"I ken that's no' what ye want to hear, but there's nae help for it, Miss LeClaire." Eyes hooded, he observed her guardedly, as if he expected her to dissolve into hysterics. An enigmatic expression flashed across his face, then was gone. "I always err on the side of prudence and safety."

And that's why he tore across the road, a gun pointed directly at him, to protect a woman he dinna ken? And why he plowed full-on into the other crazed driver wieldin' a knife?

Summoning prudence, she held her tongue and wandered to the fireplace to stare into the dying blaze. God help her.

Shutting her eyes, Emeline strove for equanimity.

She was in a hunting lodge. In the middle of the woods. Somewhere in the Scottish Highlands. With a striking, rather intimidating stranger.

It wasn't that she feared Liam MacKay. She didn't.

Opening her eyes, she accepted that truth. If he'd meant her harm, he'd had plenty of opportunities already.

Still, she couldn't deny their forced situation unnerved her. Not a soul knew where she was. Not that anyone would care, other than her friends, Berget Jonston—soon to be Berget Kennedy—and Arieen Wallace.

A few flames valiantly flickered in the fireplace, greedily consuming the single charred log remaining. Did Emeline dare ask to add another to the fire?

No, he might think her a demanding female, and she'd already been trial enough for him. Besides, she preferred cool chambers. Their apartments in Edinburgh only had coal stoves in the modiste shop's main room and the upstairs kitchen.

Naturally, Emeline's reputation already teetered on the fringe of ruin. But that didn't bother her as much as it might have another. A woman in her position—illegitimate and without a dowry—didn't have to fret about marriage offers. Or the lack thereof.

In fact, until recently, when Aunt Jeneva had suggested Emeline might consider a union with a distant cousin, marriage had never been mentioned.

She'd assumed her spinster aunt expected her to follow in her footsteps and remain unwed. That wasn't what she wanted, but, if nothing else, Emeline faced facts straight on. A husband and children weren't things she'd likely ever have.

She'd ceased mourning for what would never be years ago.

Yes, she claimed a disgraced French count as her maternal grandfather, but she wasn't respectable according to Society's strictures. Neither was she of the lower orders. What she was —and would always be—was a woman suspended between two worlds and fitting into neither. Unwanted by both. An outcast.

He shifted impatiently.

She realized, absorbed in her ruminations, that she hadn't responded. "I'm sure ye ken best, Baron." In this, she'd have to trust him. Odd that she did, but did she have any choice?

A rough noise echoed in the back of his throat as he swept his hand in a dismissive gesture, his mouth skewing into a slightly mocking smile. "Call me, Liam."

Nae. That would be highly improper.

He twisted to look out the window again, his demeanor pensive as he scraped a hand through his glossy ink-black hair. What did he seek or expect to see in the impenetrable blackness?

Mentally shrugging, she directed her focus to the struggling fire once more. The flames calmed and relaxed her, and she blinked sleepily.

"I ken ye'd prefer to return to Killeaggian Tower," he said, a trace of regret in his burr. "But 'tis a full day's journey on ideal roads. My home is closer, so we'll travel there. Once we arrive, ye can pen a letter to whoever ye need to contact and let them ken what has occurred."

"There isna anyone." Mouth pulled into a firm line, absent of self-pity, Emeline glanced over her shoulder. "I suppose I should let Berget and Arieen ken, but I ken verra little about my aunt and mother's French relatives."

She turned to face him fully and adjusted the blanket around her shoulders again, enjoying the meager fire's heat warming her back. A distinct pre-dawn chill had invaded the cottage.

As if sensing her need, he crossed to the hearth and knelt,

placing two more logs on the fire. At once, the flames greedily licked up the sides of the additional wood.

His back muscles bunched and flexed as he stoked the blaze, and she had the oddest desire to run her hands over the taut, suntanned flesh. He bore another six-inch scar under his right arm, and two smaller jagged lines stood out starkly, one on his left shoulder and the other just above his left hip.

He was a man accustomed to physical exertion and, evidently, defending himself.

"I'll need to return to Edinburgh and go through my aunt's possessions and papers. Perhaps there's an address or a letter...or somethin'." She pulled her eyebrows together as another thought intruded. "I suppose I'll need to speak to a solicitor as well."

How much would that cost?

Aunt Jeneva had money hidden in a leather bag beneath a floorboard in the shop. She'd believed it safer there than in their apartments above the business or a bank. "I dinna even ken if my aunt had a will or who inherits. I always assumed that I would, but I dinna ken for certain."

She really shouldn't be speaking so freely to him.

Normally, shyness had her stumbling over her words. Honestly, this was the longest conversation she'd ever had with a man, thanks to Aunt Jeneva's hawk-like watchfulness. Emeline had secretly assumed her aunt feared she'd make the same colossal mistake her mother had.

He gave a sympathetic nod, his shoulder-length hair swinging from the motion. Bright strands of silver glittered throughout his hair, giving him a rakish, swashbuckler air.

Wasn't he a bit young to be graying already?

How old was he anyway?

Berget hadn't mentioned his age. Studying his face, noting the subtle creases, Emeline judged him to be early in his fourth decade.

"Dinna fash yerself. There will be time to work out all the details later." Fine lines framed his kind steel-gray eyes beneath straight ebony brows. He curved his molded mouth upward, and her stomach flip-flopped.

When he smiled...

Lord, help her. It was as if the sun dropped from the heavens and lit the room. He transformed from wildly rugged to downright beautiful. It was all she could do not to gawk like a green schoolgirl.

"Emeline?"

She closed her eyes, savoring her name spoken in his melodic baritone. How could he make the word sound so lovely? She'd never been particularly fond of her given name but uttered from his lips, it became quite wonderful. Even if he did overstep addressing her by her given name without her consent.

"Do ye have any idea why those men wanted to kill ye?" he gently probed.

Lifting her eyelids, she shook her head.

He shrewdly observed her, and although he remained outwardly relaxed, she didn't miss the intensity in his gaze or the edge of tension in his shoulders. She'd wager his jaw had hardened beneath that bushy beard too.

Remembered terror overwhelmed her for an instant, and she closed her eyes until the wave of nausea and fear passed. Opening her eyelids, she sought his reassuring gaze and lifted a shoulder. "Nae. We're no' wealthy, nor do we possess chests of jewels and the like. I think it must've been a case of mistaken identity. There can be nae other reason."

Thank God Liam had killed the blackguards so they couldn't carry out their despicable mission on their true target.

"They kent yer name, lass." He rubbed his cheek. "It wasna a mistake."

She snapped her gaze back to his, and her jaw went slack. Amid the horror and chaos, she'd forgotten that indisputable fact.

Compassion softened his craggy features, and he touched a curl laying atop her shoulder, the gesture at odds with his warrior's bearing. "They also said they'd been paid to do the deed. Are ye sure ye have nae enemies?"

The tress coiled lovingly around his forefinger, the brazen thing.

"Nae. None. We've lived a quiet life, only attendin' an occasional dance or assembly. The trip to Killeaggian Tower was the first time I've left Edinburgh in my entire life." She brushed her fingertips across one eye. "I canna believe any of this has happened. It makes nae sense."

The ordeal had left her terrified and confused. Her whole world had tilted on its axis, and she'd no way to right it. Didn't even know where to begin or who she could trust except Liam MacKay.

"We'll get to the bottom of it," he assured her, confident and certain. "Dinna fash yerself."

How could she not worry?

He was right, nevertheless. The men *had* known her name, and they'd taken the place of the real drivers.

Had they killed them too?

Come to think of it, *should* she return to Edinburgh?

If someone was determined to dispose of her, wouldn't they expect her to do that very thing? She'd have to rethink that decision. Perhaps Liam might have a suggestion about how best to proceed, although imposing upon him further seemed presumptuous.

"Ye're frettin'. I see it in yer doe eyes. No' can be done now." He gently turned her toward the bunk and gave her a wee shove. "Now back to bed with ye. It will be dawn in a few hours, and I plan on goin' huntin' first thing. If I'm nae here when ye wake, dinna worry."

How had he known that was precisely what she'd have done?

He gestured to the overflowing shelves. "There's makin's for coffee and tea and porridge. Help yerself. Och, and the necessary is out back. There's a brook nearby too."

"This place is for huntin', I take it?" Giving him a small upward sweep of her mouth, she shuffled to her hard, narrow bed, and he did likewise.

"Aye. Several of my friends, includin' Graeme Kennedy, Broden McGregor, Quinn Catherwood, and Coburn Wallace use it." Only Graeme Kennedy and Coburn Wallace's names were familiar to her.

"We built it ourselves as teenagers." He sighed as he relaxed onto the thin mattress. The cot groaned under his weight as he yawned. "Monthly, we rotate who checks the place and makes sure basic supplies are on hand. One never kens when one might have the urge to get away for a time."

Or save a woman from would-be-assassins and a flash flood.

Emeline settled onto her side, drowsily staring at him. She owed this stranger much. If he hadn't intervened—

She closed her eyes and gave her head a little shake to dislodge the gruesome image. "Liam?"

"Aye?" His bed squeaked as he changed position, so he, too, lay on his side. He barely fit in his bunk, however. Evidently, the teenage boys who'd built the cottage hadn't considered how much larger they'd be as grown men.

How odd it was to be a few feet away from a man she scarcely knew, both of them abed and wearing next to nothing. Yet, she wasn't the least afraid. There was an aura about Liam MacKay, an invisible wall, despite his gentleness and chivalry.

"Thank ye, again," she murmured, emotion tightening her chest. "I truly do owe ye my life, and I ken I've put ye to a deal of trouble. If it werena for me, ye'd be home by now."

To his waiting wife?

Was that why he'd not made any improper advances? He was married and faithful to his wife, as well? If so, that raised him further in her estimation. She'd met few inherently decent men of his caliber.

Or, perchance, he found her lacking. Most men did. That knowledge didn't bring the sting it once did. Girlish fantasies fade, and life's realities toughen sensible women.

"I'm just glad I was there and able to help," he murmured sleepily. "Now rest, lass. Ye've had a tremendous shock."

She had, but knowing he was just a few feet away brought her much relief. Else she'd not have been able to sleep a wink. Closing her eyes, she snuggled further beneath the blanket.

"Emeline?"

"Hmm?" It was much too great an effort to open her eyes again.

"I think ye'd better plan on stayin' at Eytone Hall, my

familial home, until we ken ye're out of danger." Was it very wrong that she found his sleepy voice sexy? "And I think ye should consider usin' a different name for a time."

Her eyelids popped open, and her gaze tangled with his across the room.

"Is that really necessary?" she whispered, fully understanding the implication of his suggestion. He believed she was in grave danger.

"Aye, and since the assassins kent yer full name, it will have to be a name they willna suspect." He brushed a hand over his beard, eyeing her speculatively. "Do ye fancy any certain name?"

Eyes partially closed, she wrinkled her nose, considering the question. "I've always liked Mareona."

He went perfectly still, his mouth drawn into a grim line and his quicksilver eyes boring into hers. Such emotion sparked in their depths, Emeline's heart skipped a painful beat.

"That...that 'twas my bairn's name."

THREE

Emeline puttered around the cottage, casting frequent glances out the dusty window. She had awoken a couple of hours ago to golden sunlight streaming into the cottage. After summoning her courage, she'd ventured outdoors and used the necessary. She didn't like the fear that had shrouded her since yesterday.

Upon returning indoors, she'd rinsed her mouth and added a log to the fire. Shivering despite the crackling blaze in the hearth, she'd quickly bathed with cold water from the bucket and soft citrus-scented soap she'd found in a jar before hastily dressing.

Grimacing, she'd donned her bloodstained traveling gown, but there'd been no help for it. Her trunk had been lost in the flood.

Drawing in a ragged sigh, she placed a palm to her forehead, as if the gesture would help steady her rioting thoughts and emotions.

She'd brought her best clothes to the gathering at Killeaggian Tower, and everything else she owned was in

Edinburgh. The minute they arrived at Liam's home, she'd borrow a gown and have this one burned.

Once again peering outdoors, she combed her fingers through her thick, unruly hair. Encountering a snarl, she winced. *Heavens.* She didn't even own a hairbrush anymore, and her hairpins had come out while she struggled against the curs hauling her and her aunt from the coach yesterday.

Continuing to work the tangles free with her fingers, she let her mind wander.

She wasn't exactly impoverished, but neither was she in an ideal position. Everything—her very future—hung upon Aunt Jeneva's will. *If* she had one. If not...

Emeline gave herself a mental shake. No sense in fretting about something she couldn't change. Satisfied she'd smoothed the worst of the knots from her hair, she searched for a length of string to tie back the fly-away mass. Finding none, she ripped a strip from her petticoat and then proceeded to gather her hair into a simple queue at her nape.

Time enough to worry about the will, or lack thereof, later. For now, she'd concentrate on the simple fare she'd prepared to break their fast while waiting for Liam to return. Thank goodness she knew how to cook, having prepared most of the meals for her and Aunt Jeneva.

While rummaging through the supplies on the shelf, she'd found dried apples and had added them to the oat porridge warming in a pot before the hearth along with a kettle of tea. Grinning in delight upon discovering a tin of yeast, she'd even managed to set bread to rise. It mightn't turn out as she'd anticipated since she didn't have eggs or milk.

Nevertheless, if they'd be stuck here for at least a day as

Liam had said, they'd not go hungry. Why, she might even try her hand at an apple tart.

Truthfully, she couldn't imagine any of the men Liam had mentioned—any man, honestly—making bread or porridge. She'd expected they'd just roasted whatever they'd killed over the fire and survived on meat while they stayed here. Nevertheless, whoever had been appointed to stock the cottage last had done an admirable job.

Resting a hip against the table beneath the window, she searched the landscape beyond and sipped the surprisingly strong and robust tea. Evidence of the storm's ravages met her scrutiny. Branches and limbs littered the ground. In the distance, several felled and uprooted trees lay at awkward angles. She could only imagine the damage from the rampaging river.

When she'd seen that frothing water bearing down upon them—her heart lurched in remembered terror—she thought she'd exchanged one hell for another. It occurred to her then, since the assassins had stopped where they did, she'd have died from the flood, as would they all have. Fate had spared her life in the form of the bear of a Highlander.

As she took another sip, Liam strode toward the cottage carrying two hares, his hair brushing his shoulders.

His plaid swished about his knees, the tartan's striking pine green and bold blue made it one of the loveliest she'd ever seen. His deep blue woolen coat emphasized his broad shoulders and, from a distance, made his eyes appear slate-blue rather than the flinty gray of the ocean before a storm. With each wide stride, his long hair caressed his shoulders, and his dark brown leather sporran bounced slightly.

He paused at a lean-to, lowering the hares to the damp

earth. His mouth turned upward affectionately, he brushed his palm over his horse's withers, speaking to the magnificent beast all the while. The massive gelding, an unusual steely silver-gray color, nudged his master's chest, and Liam chuckled.

Teacup halfway to her mouth, Emeline gasped, sloshing a splash of the warm brew onto the bodice of her gown. *Och, my goodness.* She hastily dabbed at the spill with a cloth.

When Liam laughed unrestrainedly, his entire countenance lit up, transforming him from a brusque, harsh man to an irresistible Grecian god. Well, if she'd ever seen a statue of Grecian or Roman god, she imagined Liam resembled one.

What would he look like shaved and his hair shorn?

She canted her head, considering him. A strong nose divided his face and, given the chiseled planes of the rest of him, he likely possessed an angular jaw and chin beneath that nest of a beard.

He'd be one of those men too handsome for words, she suspected. But there was a guardedness about him, an aloofness. A stay-at-arms-length reserve, even while he'd held her in his embrace comforting her last night.

She'd noticed it before too.

At Killeaggian Tower, he'd kept to himself during the celebration.

No, that wasn't entirely true.

He'd mingled with the men, laughing and joking, quaffing back pints of ale. But whenever an unwed woman approached, except for his spirited sister, he'd all but pelted in the other direction, sword drawn.

The table's edge biting into the flesh of her hip, she shifted her position and narrowed her eyes. There was much about the enigmatic Baron Penderhaven she didn't know or understand, but she was honest enough to admit he'd stirred her curiosity and heretofore undecipherable longings. Illicit and immoral longings, given he was a married man.

"That was my bairn's name."

Was, not is. How had she died?

Such pain had permeated his ragged voice that she'd immediately elected to use Margaret instead. God knew Margarets abounded in Scotland, as common as red squirrels, heather, and the mountain hares he'd snared today.

Last night, without another word, he'd turned his broad back to her. Feeling like she'd committed a breach of etiquette, she'd faced the opposite wall as well. Exhaustion soon overtook her, and she'd tumbled into a deep, but decidedly unpeaceful, sleep.

As she took another swallow of the rather good tea, she furled her forehead. Why hadn't Liam's wife accompanied him to the *cèilidh*?

Perhaps she was unwell, or she didn't like social gatherings. Or mayhap, they didn't get on well together. No one had mentioned he was married. Not Berget and not his sister, Kendra. Emeline had liked and admired Kendra instantly. Confident, kind, full of life, and a bit mischievous, she was so very different than her somber brother.

So very different than Emeline too.

After another pat to the horse's side, Liam collected the hares. He glanced toward the cottage, and his gaze locked with hers through the dingy glass as he slowly straightened to his full several inches over six-foot height.

Emeline couldn't pull her attention away and, across the span, something powerful and unnamable sparked between them. An invisible bond that speared straight to her soul took root there.

It was wrong. *Verra wrong.* He was married. Yet she could not avert her gaze.

To her consternation, Liam glanced away first, and strange disappointment tunneled through her. Flames licking her cheeks, she hurriedly spun from the window and made her way to the table. She placed her cup beside a bowl. She'd no business noticing a man's looks or paying attention to disturbing flutters behind her breastbone and in her stomach.

For God's sake. Her aunt had died yesterday. Men had tried to kill her. She had no idea what the future held. What she did know without a doubt was it did not include the brawny Highlander who'd saved her.

He. Is. Married.

A half-dozen breaths later, the door swung open, and he entered. At once, his presence filled the space. He lifted the hares, a hint of pride sharpening his already hewn features. "I need to tend to these, but I wanted to make sure ye didna need anythin' first."

"Nae, nothin'." Although she was grateful for the meat, she couldn't help but feel a twinge of sadness for the sweet creatures.

"I did see several red deer today, but we canna eat one between us, and I willna wantonly hunt and waste the meat." His cheeks slightly ruddy from the wind, he jerked his strong chin. "Between hares, fish from the brook, and grouse, I'll keep ye well-fed."

Emeline had never doubted it. Liam MacKay seemed most capable of fending for himself and those under his care.

"I have tea and porridge ready, and bread is risin' too." She swept a hand toward the hearth. "Would ye like to eat first, and then perhaps ye can show me how to skin and clean the hares?"

His gypsy-dark eyebrows shuffled high onto his noble brow. "Ye want to learn to clean hares?" He appeared so astounded, she might've asked him to dance a jig naked in the snow while playing the bagpipes. His blatant amazement stirred unexpected resentment and chagrin.

"Ye dinna have to teach me if ye dinna want to." She wasn't exactly keen to learn to skin the animals in any event. Nevertheless, for some unfathomable reason, she wanted him to understand she wasn't cossetted or pampered. Wishing to steer the conversation in another direction, she said, "I assume ye snared them?"

"Aye."

"I'd like to learn how to set a snare too." And with that imprudent candidness, she'd trod right back into the quagmire.

He placed the hares on the floor and, still eyeing her curiously, also set aside his sword and dirk. Befuddlement reshaping his countenance and three lines creasing his forehead, he shook his head slowly. "I think perhaps, Miss Emeline LeClaire, ye're the most unique woman I've ever met."

Not altogether certain he'd meant the observation as a compliment, she pinched her lips together. "Why? Because I asked ye to teach me to clean the hares?" She hitched a shoulder, feigning a nonchalance she was far from feeling. "Honestly, I think it's a skill that I might have use of someday. One never kens what life might throw at ye."

Hadn't they seen that firsthand yesterday? And today as well?

His eyebrows scuttled higher as he settled himself into the chair opposite her. "Forgive me for bein' obtuse, but I canna imagine the need ever arisin'."

Because she wasn't quite a lady of station, but neither was she a farmer's wife required to kill and pluck her chickens? He didn't know that though. Stifling the terse retort tapping her teeth, Emeline turned her attention to breaking their fast.

She had no quarrel with him. She *was* grateful for all he'd done for her. It wasn't his fault she found herself in this impossible situation. He'd been all that was gallant. If he believed the chore too distasteful for her to learn, then she wasn't going to kick up a fuss about it.

After using a cloth to bring the porridge and tea kettle to the table, she settled into a chair, her hands on either side of her bowl. She was famished, not having eaten since yesterday morning.

"Never mind. It was a foolish thing to ask," Emeline said, dropping her gaze.

Liam placed one hand over hers, giving her fingers a minute squeeze. He then turned her hand over and traced his forefinger over the pads. A jolt of sensual awareness traveled from her palm up her forearm to her shoulder, and heat blossomed across her chest before hurtling up her neck and face.

A simple, innocent touch. Tantalizing. Tempting.

The inarguable physical attraction to him bewildered and alarmed her. No man had ever set her—sensible and reticent Emeline LeClaire—pulse to cavorting. This wasn't wise. He was a married man. They were unchaperoned.

Her heightened senses were due to the scare she'd suffered yesterday. The primitive need to survive. Wasn't it normal for people thrust into dire circumstances together to form a connection? A bond borne of forced company? It didn't mean it accounted for anything.

With his next words, all of her rational arguments scattered like thistledown in a gale.

"Ye're a gentlewoman. These soft hands are no' meant for menial labor, lass. Neither are they meant to be covered with blood and gore." He slanted his arresting blue gaze to the now-empty clothesline. "Ye were wearin' gloves yesterday. Women who skin hares and set snares dinna even own a pair of gloves."

The last held a measure of steel and censure, and she wasn't altogether certain he still spoke about her. Nonetheless, smothering a barbed response, she snatched her hands away as if scorched. Scowling, she lifted her forearms and spread her fingers.

"These hands are for whatever I need to do to survive, Baron." She speared him a reproving glare, not quite understanding why his words had angered her. "I've been sewin' with *these hands* since I could hold a needle at the age of five. I kept my aunt's house, cooked for us, ordered her supplies, and maintained the books for her business. True, I've no' done much menial labor, but I am no' above soilin' *these hands*. My life has been neither easy nor pampered. After the events of yesterday, I have nae doubt it has become vastly more difficult."

"Emeline, I meant nae offense." He looked taken aback, and a hint of remorse turned his firm mouth downward.

A mouth she very much would like to kiss. That realization shocked and thrilled.

"Didna ye?" she said, spooning porridge into his bowl, then hers with short, terse movements.

"Nae, and I beg yer pardon." He sighed and scrubbed a

hand through his hair. "I only meant ye dinna have to lower yerself to such a task. 'Tis nae pleasant, even for a seasoned hunter such as me." He accepted the cup of tea she shoved his way, then pointed a thumb over his shoulder.

She tracked her attention to the hares before quickly looking away.

"I saw the way ye looked at the wee things," he said. "Ye've a soft heart, and there's nothin' wrong with that. Ye've been through a terrible trauma. I'd no' add teachin' ye how to skin and clean an animal to yer burden right now."

Despite her stern admonishments, she felt her ire and humiliation melting away. She could almost believe Liam was genuinely concerned.

Imprudent warmth bloomed in her heart.

"Ye need time to heal." He winked, and her heart stopped for a full beat. "At Eytone Hall, if ye're still of a mind to learn, I'll teach ye."

FOUR

Liam ran a hand over his beard. Of late, he'd actually contemplated shaving it off. Kristin had despised facial hair. After she'd scarred his face, he'd grown the beard, partially to conceal the scar, but primarily to rile her.

With deliberate intent, he shoved thoughts of his unhappy, dead wife aside. She'd haunted his dreams and memories long enough. From beneath half-closed eyes, he watched Emeline pick at her breakfast.

What in the name of the wee man had possessed him to claim she wasn't meant for menial tasks? He'd sounded like an arrogant, condescending arse. Anyone with eyes in their head could see she wasn't a pampered lass in manner or appearance.

The color still high on her cheeks, and what he suspected was hurt shimmering in those gorgeous big doe eyes of hers, she gave a slight shake of her dark head. "Let's no' argue. Ye're right. I dinna want to perform the task. I just wanted to show that I was capable and have nae need to be waited upon."

Lifting the cup, he took an appreciative sip while studying

her. Why did she feel a need to prove herself? He hadn't paid her much mind at Kennedy's gathering, but from what he *had* observed, she appeared timid and retiring.

He didn't recall her dancing or even speaking to any men for that matter. But that might've been due to her dragon of an aunt hovering about and breathing fire at any gentleman who glanced at Emeline with more than passing interest.

Why wasn't she married?

Why did he care?

He didn't. And with that determined and final thought, he turned his attention to his cooling porridge. Taking a bite, he opened his eyes wide in surprise. "Ye put apples in the porridge?"

She gave him a searching look and then a hesitant nod. "Aye. I thought they'd add a bit of flavor."

"It's delicious."

This time, a flush of pleasure turned her cheeks rosy, and when she dropped her umber-eyed gaze to her bowl, a slight, pleased smile bent her pink lips upward. "I thought, if ye'd like, that is, I could make an apple tart or pie this afternoon. I found a small sugar cone but nae spices."

An apple pie?

Odin's balls, he adored apple pie.

Why wasn't this jewel of a woman married?

Were all men in Edinburgh blind, daft idiots?

The prices of spices were far too dear to leave them in an unattended cottage. However, Liam adored apple anything. Had since he was a wee laddie.

"I'd be most grateful for a pie," he said with a wink.

She appeared inexplicably pleased by his response and gifted him with a celestial smile.

His heart leaped behind his ribcage, shaking his judiciously erected ramparts of isolation and aloofness. If he wasn't diligent, this entrancing lass might very well cause the formerly impenetrable battlements he'd come to rely upon to crumble to fine dust at his feet.

Mustering his equanimity, he helped himself to another serving of porridge, then casually glanced about the small cottage. He couldn't count the number of times he'd come here with his friends or by himself.

Especially when Kristin was alive but before the wee bairns came along. He'd needed the respite from her incessant nagging, harping, and complaining. Never had he known such a discontented woman. Nothing pleased her and, even now, nine years after meeting her, he still couldn't believe he'd been stupid enough to be caught in her well-devised trap.

He'd not so easily slip into a harness again.

Liam took another bite and, chewing thoughtfully, observed the woman across from him.

Emeline LeClaire was the opposite of his deceased wife in almost every way.

As dark in coloring as Kristin had been fair. As slender and lithe as Kristin had been abundantly rounded in all the places men most appreciated. As soft-spoken, serene, and considerate as Kristin had been demanding, difficult, and impossible to please. As unassuming and unaware of her loveliness as Kristin had been bold and confident of her unquestionable allure.

Once before, beauty and lust had blinded him.

And where, devil it, had that landed him?

Never again would he lose control or be vulnerable to a woman's wiles. Having one's heart carved out with a bejeweled hairpin and the remnants left for the crows to feast upon rather had a way of discouraging interest or affection for the fairer sex.

Except his mother and sister, naturally.

"I only walked a few miles huntin' this mornin', but that storm caused a significant amount of devastation. More than I estimated." He angled his spoon toward the window. "I saw more than one mudslide, and, in all honesty, Emeline, I wouldna be surprised if the road hasna washed out."

She darted a glance outside before bringing her attention back to him, infinite patience in her whisky-colored eyes. Instinct told him she'd make a superb mother.

Hold there, he silently chastised himself. Emeline might be a beguiling lass, but musings about motherhood were too bloody intimate for his comfort.

He cleared his throat. "I ken I told ye we'd need to stay for a day, but I dinna think it would be wise to leave for at least three."

Hooking an arm over the back of his chair, Liam instinctively braced himself for a fit of high-pitched, tear-laced feminine displeasure.

Rather than becoming upset about the delay in their departure, Emeline regarded him serenely. "I noticed the degree of damage in the nearby woodlands."

Och, aye. Before him was the calm, self-possessed Miss LeClaire.

He relaxed under the knowledge she wasn't given to histrionics. "The ground's saturated and unstable and requires time to dry. I'm nae takin' a chance of travelin' on sodden earth that may give way beneath us."

Thank all the saints, this wasn't a woman accustomed to flying into fits of temper. He had known her for less than a day but already knew she thought things through with tranquil logic.

"Ye ken the area, Liam. And as ye are more accustomed to travelin' by horseback through this type of terrain, I canna but concede to yer wisdom." She glanced over her shoulder toward the foodstuffs on the shelf. "We've sufficient food, the brook for water, and wood for the fire. We shall be fine."

"Indeed, we shall." He found her bravado irrationally endearing. He also found the idea of spending time alone with her in this isolated cottage far more appealing than he ought to.

Dinna let yer guard down.

Truth to tell, there was much about Emeline LeClaire to admire. Not the least of which was her creamy complexion and luxurious bronze hair. Not quite copper and not quite sable, it shimmered with a light of its own. Her winged eyebrows and lush lashes were several shades darker and combined with her doe eyes, created an aura of warm richness around her.

It comforted and beckoned to him in a way he couldn't begin to understand but which slightly terrified as much as mesmerized.

She swept her unusual amber-toned gaze about the cottage before turning those beguiling eyes on him.

He recognized that redolent look, and the gnarled knot that was his stomach pulled tighter.

It was the look a woman gave a man when she meant to ask for something. Kristin had mastered the art with dimple-producing coy smiles and a provocative turn of her neck or sweep of her hand across her ample bosom.

"I dinna suppose ye've a hip bath somewhere?" Emeline ventured hopefully. Bashfully.

A rosy hue mounted her porcelain cheeks, and Liam almost choked on an incredulous laugh. *That's what she wanted?* God's teeth, he'd become jaded. "Nae. We usually bathe in the brook." If they bathed at all, freezing cold though it might be. The men didn't come here for comfort or niceties.

She valiantly curved her lips upward, notching her higher in his estimation.

"I shall make do with the bucket just fine." Fingering a lock of hair, she eyed the pail. Was she pondering how to wash her hair? He could offer to help, but he didn't trust himself to touch her so intimately.

At once, images invaded his mind of her naked before the fireplace, her pearly skin iridescent from the candles' glow, and water trickling over that satiny flesh as she bathed.

His body reacted to the erotic conjuring, and he shifted in his seat as he gulped down a swallow of tepid tea. The next few days were going to be pure torture. He'd best keep himself occupied outdoors cleaning up after the storm and chopping wood.

Yes. Just the thing for a randy Highlander with a beauty sharing his much-too-small cottage. Whose bloody damn drunken idea was it to build such a wee hunting lodge?

She brushed a tendril of her burnished chestnut hair over her shoulder, the movement graceful and completely unaffected. Unfortunately, it pulled her bodice tight and drew Liam's gaze to the forbidden mounds.

Wood choppin'. Cuttin' trees down. Stackin' wood.

There was a bloody forest outside. He'd chop enough firewood to keep the lodge heated until the next century if it kept him out of the cottage. Kept him away from this alluring woman with her innocent, seductive eyes the color of caramelized sugar. Then he'd fall into bed so exhausted each night that dreams wouldn't even disturb his slumber, let alone a lithe siren enticing him in ways that hadn't tempted in years.

After a frigid soak in yonder stream.

They finished their simple meal in silence, and just as he was about to ask if she'd like to take a walk, she blurted, "I'm so verra sorry about yer daughter."

Liam clasped his hand so tightly around his spoon, his knuckles turned white as he clamped his jaw against the grief that yet possessed the ability to steal his breath and stall his lungs. "She's been gone for over five years." He hadn't meant to share something so private with her. He didn't discuss his children with anyone, not even his mother or sister.

It was simply too damned gut-wrenchingly painful. Countless times, his mother had begged him to talk about the bairns. She vowed he couldn't keep the grief pent up inside; that it would corrode away at him from the inside and destroy his soul.

Kendra had said the same, and even though he knew his mother and sister mourned too, he couldn't talk about the tragedy that had stolen both of his beloved bairns the same day. The calamity that would never have happened if he'd been the father he should've been. If he'd protected them instead of being compassionate.

God, even now, he wanted to smash his fist into the wall and keen his anguish.

Last night, when Emeline had picked the same name as his daughter's, her choice had so stunned him that he'd blurted that Mareona had been his bairn's name. His wee cherub of a son, scarcely one year old, had been called Joseph.

Each child had possessed their mother's golden hair but his slate-gray eyes. And he'd adored them beyond comprehension. Hadn't known he was capable of that depth of love and devotion. Even thinking about them now brought a rush of biting moisture to his eyes.

"I'm sure ye understand if I dinna want to talk about it," he mumbled.

The plump pillows of her lush lips thinning, she conceded with a slight dip of her dainty chin. "Aye, I can understand. No' about losin' a child, because I've never had a bairn, but I do ken about losin' a relative. Every time it's brought up, it feels as if the wound has reopened."

"Aye." And he feared he'd never heal. He'd never be whole again. Never see a wee blond girl or boy and not feel as if his heart and lungs were being torn from his chest. He never, ever wanted to feel that kind of pain again.

He glanced at the window and the vivid blue sky shimmering between the greenish-black treetops. Such a contrast to the hellish heavens that had buffeted them yesterday. But then again, he lived in a sort of hell for five years now.

Suspended in place, mourning. *Always—God help me— mournin'*. He couldn't seem to move on, to put aside his anger.

Such scorching anger.

At Kristin, the devil's daughter. At God. At himself for yielding to the temptation that fateful night nine years ago and accepting the invitation he naively believed she offered. Only to learn it had been a calculated trap. He'd been played like a gullible, malleable fool all along.

His appetite gone, he pushed the bowl away and took up the cup of tea. Apparently, the same was true for Emeline, for she leaned back in her chair, her cup poised near her soft lips.

"Have ye any other children?" she softly asked, a hint of hesitancy in her husky voice.

Closing his eyes for an agonizing blink, Liam swore a thousand curses beneath his breath. "I had a son."

As comprehension dawned, the air exploded from her in a harsh whoosh. "Och, my God, Liam." She thumped her cup down hard, jostling the table. "Please dinna tell me ye lost him *too*?" Her words emerged strangled and tight, as if tears and emotion clogged her throat.

He couldn't look at her. Couldn't stand to see his anguish reflected in her tormented eyes. Instead, he stared fixedly at the coin-sized stain beside his cup. "Aye. At the same time."

Her harsh respiration slashed his heart. His composure.

He glanced up then, knowing he'd see pity and sympathy and compassion. They only fueled his agony. His mother and sister, friends, the clan members, the staff at Eytone Hall, the tenants and villagers—all had turned that sorrowful, helpless expression on him hundreds and hundreds of times.

Odin's teeth, he'd been offered platitudes and condolences and banalities and commiserations until he wanted to break something. To smash his fists into a stone wall and tear the pennants and portraits from Eytone Hall's galleys. To shout his rage to the heavens until he grew hoarse.

But none of that would help.

Nothing...*nothing* would repair Joseph's and Mareona's wee broken bodies.

He'd never again see their precious faces light up as they giggled or smell their sweet essence as he held them, his face nestled in their downy hair. Never grin as they capered about the house and lawns, or sigh in immeasurable contentment as they snuggled on his lap.

Shaking her head, her eyes luminous, Emeline put a trembling hand to her bosom. "My heart aches mightily for ye, Liam. Words canna express my sorrow," she whispered brokenly. "How ye and yer wife must suffer."

He lowered his brows thunderously, familiar bitter lines hardening his face as he slammed his fist upon the table, rattling the dishes and utensils.

Emeline jumped, her expression equal parts dismay and confusion.

His good sense and control had flown in the face of the rage resulting from Kristin's actions. Rancor made his voice razor-sharp. "My wife is dead. I dinna ever speak of her. *Ever.*"

Lower lip trembling, her face white as the lace edging her bodice, Emeline swallowed. Her doe eyes huge and alarmed, she regarded him warily before casting a less-than-covert glance toward the door. She thought him utterly and completely mad.

He *had* been off his head for the first few weeks after his children's deaths.

Gaze leery, she folded her hands, shadows of doubt and fear stamped upon her face.

Dammit. Now Liam had succeeded in frightening her.

But ever since yesterday, he'd been thrown into a lather. He despised this lack of self-control. Loathed *feeling*. Sighing, he scraped a hand over his eyes. "Forgive me. 'Tis no' somethin' I can speak of or think about without becomin' angry. But ye're in nae danger from me, lass. I give ye my word."

Marked uncertainty was engraved upon her features. "I

believe that's for me to decide, and in order to do so, I fear, I shall have to impose upon ye further." Her eyes the color of warm dark honey, she courageously notched her small chin slightly higher.

No' so brave, after all.

"How..." She licked her lower lip. "How did they die?"

FIVE

The fraught silence stretched onward, the initial uncomfortable sliver lengthening into an unspoken challenge. A challenge Liam knew for damned certain he'd lost. *Shite.* With a grumbled oath, Liam slouched against his chair.

He wouldn't put it past the enigmatic Emeline LeClaire to set out on her own if he didn't answer. And by damn, he hadn't risked his life to have her break her dainty neck haring about these storm-ravaged woodlands. However, for this unwelcome conversation, he'd need something significantly stronger than tea.

He wrested his flask from his coat pocket. After taking a long swallow—relishing the steady, bracing burn to his gut— he set the silver container atop the table. He didn't bother putting the cap back on, since he knew full well he'd likely finish the contents. He also knew there were two bottles of whisky and another two of brandy at the back of the top shelf. After all, he'd seen the cottage supplied last.

If he were alone, he'd likely drink himself into oblivion.

Something he'd done far too much of over these past few years. A habit he'd vowed nearly daily to stop, to cease giving Kristin that kind of power over him. But grief, hatred, bitterness, heartbreak, and despair were much easier to face with a dram or two of strong spirits dulling one's senses.

So was the knowledge he'd never see his wee darlings again.

Schooling his features into a mask of indifference he was far from feeling, as the fury yet fulminating in his veins testified, he regarded Emeline coolly.

She met his gaze straight on, her eyes bright and clear.

Again, he admired her pluck. Men generally cowed from him when he leveled his frigid glare upon them.

"My wife was English," he said, the words bitter upon his tongue. "A Sassenach from Kent. The short story is that after trickin' me into marryin' her, and nearly four years of livin' in the Highlands, she decided it wasna the life for her after all. One day in early January, when I took several of my clansmen to deal with marauders on the northern border, she packed our children into a travelin' coach, intent on returnin' to her parents in England."

He stared at the table, absently noting the many scratches and grooves from the fifteen plus years of him and his friends using the place. He ran his forefinger over a deep indentation, which, if he recalled correctly, was a result of Broden McGregor's cutting a stag hide.

"I returned three days later after havin' chased the bandits from my lands. To my absolute dismay, I learned the coach carryin' Kristin and our children had overturned on a particularly treacherous stretch of road less than ten miles from Eytone Hall. I have nae idea why she chose that circuitous route in the winter." He rubbed a hand over his eyes. "Unless to deliberately evade me."

He'd never forced her to his bed. Never laid a hand upon her in anger. Never demanded she assume the duties of the lady of the house or visit the tenants or villagers. Kristin had been a pampered, self-indulgent termagant.

Dragging his gaze upward, he recognized his own misery reflected in Emeline's incandescent eyes. A tear leaked from the corner of hers and dribbled down her cheek.

She made no effort to wipe it away. "And...they *all* died?"

Giving a terse nod, he swallowed against the boulder in his throat. "Aye. The coach rolled several times. All were lost, includin' her maid, the coachmen, and the team."

Lower lip clamped between her neat white teeth, she slanted her head, emphasizing the elegant lines of her neck and shoulders. She was all grace and loveliness, yet she seemed wholly unaware of her subtle appeal.

Emeline's was a gentle beauty, like that of a candle's soft glow on a sleeping bairn's face, rather than the vibrant hues of a glorious sunset or sunrise upon a loch. One branded the heart, the other the soul.

"Thank ye for tellin' me, Liam, and please forgive me for insistin' ye reveal somethin' so terribly painful to a woman ye dinna ken." She knuckled away the moisture from the corner of her eyes. "I ken my words dinna help ease yer pain, but I am verra sorry ye have suffered so. I'd have gone mad with the grief."

He was still half-mad after five years. When would he heal? Would he ever? Was this to be his existence for the rest of his life, only half-alive?

Moody? Angry? Bitter?

"Thank ye," he solemnly said. In some small way, it had helped to tell her. But he feared he might've uncorked a bottle, and now there'd be no way in hell of stopping the contents from gushing forth.

Her expression at once despondent and compassionate, she pushed her chair back. "I...I should check the bread."

"And I'll take care of the hares." He stood as well. At the door, he paused. "Emeline?"

"Aye?" Holding the bowl with the bread dough in one hand, she glanced over her slender shoulder.

Liam reached into his sporran and withdrew an embroidered velvet coin purse. As he did so, she straightened and faced him, wonderment softening her features.

"I collected this yesterday," he said, crossing to her in three paces. "I placed yer aunt's earrin's inside too." The woman hadn't been wearing any other jewelry but the simple pearl earrings. The pretty fallal was another reminder Emeline had lost everything, including any valuables in her luggage.

Her expression a mélange of sanguinity and melancholy, she set the dough aside and accepted the small gold purse. After a moment's hesitation, she opened the clasp. What might've been relief flickered over her face.

She lifted a chatelain with keys from the copper-colored silk lining the purse. "I worried the keys to my home and the shop had been lost in the flood. I didna ken how I would open either. Thank ye for thinkin' to grab this and my aunt's earbobs too. She wore them every day. They were a gift from her father."

She gave him a fragile, watery smile.

Without conscious thought, Liam brushed the moisture from beneath her eye with his thumb pad and framed her jaw between his fingers with the other. "It pains me to see ye so sad."

Her mouth parted on a silent, sharp inhalation, and his attention dropped to her lips. God and all the divine powers, how he wanted to kiss those soft, pink lips.

"Liam?" she whispered breathlessly. Achingly. Invitingly.

Nae. NAE!

Wrenching his hand away as if scorched, he spun on his heel and seized the hares before stomping from the cottage. If he weren't halfway to numpty before, spending several more days alone with Emeline would drive him to the brink.

Already, his whole body hummed, responding to her, and he'd revealed more about the deaths of his bairns to her than anyone. As if compelled by a force far more powerful than him, he speared a glance to the window, half-expecting to see her on the other side.

Instead, only the sun's golden hues reflected on the dusty panes.

"Emeline," he muttered ferociously beneath his breath. "I canna let ye past my guards. I canna."

I willna.

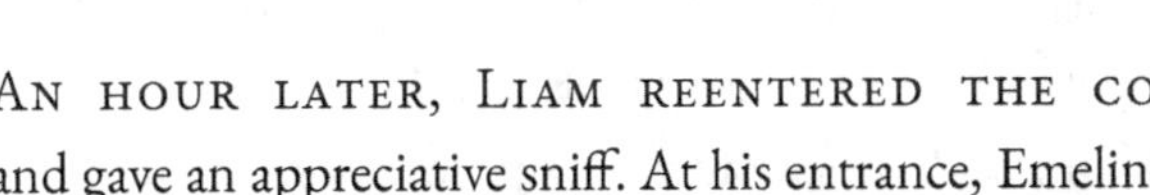

AN HOUR LATER, LIAM REENTERED THE COTTAGE and gave an appreciative sniff. At his entrance, Emeline smiled a trifle tentatively and hopeful as well. It seemed he'd put their encounter behind him and had returned to the coolly polite stranger she'd first met.

With some effort, she'd corralled her overwrought emotions and made every effort to appear as composed as him.

When he'd brushed his thumb across her face, an overpowering desire to throw her arms around him and snuggle into the comfort of his lean, honed chest had burrowed through her.

Only by biting the inside of her cheek and admonishing herself to behave like a gentle-bred young woman Aunt Jeneva would be proud of did she manage to subdue the wanton urge.

What was it about this Highland warrior that had her responding so irrationally? So uncharacteristically impulsively?

His tramping from the cottage, looking as if she'd propositioned him, stung her pride more than a kernel. She eyed the two misshapen loaves of golden-crusted bread. They might not be pretty or perfect, but she was proud of her efforts. Beside them, she'd placed a plate, a knife, and a jar of jam.

"There isna any butter, but I found preserves if ye'd like a slice," she offered by way of a truce.

A boyish grin wreathed his handsome face and, again, she pondered the transformation of his features. When happy, he was simply breathtaking. Perhaps it was because she'd had so little interaction with men—specifically, a particularly muscular Highland baron—or that they'd been thrust together, but an indescribable magnetism drew her to him.

After placing the rabbit meat atop a plate he took from the shelf, he cut a thick slice of warm bread. He slathered it with preserves and took a healthy bite. Appreciation shone in his eyes. "How did ye learn to make bread over an open fire?"

"Aunt Jeneva wasna always a successful modiste. For years, we lived in a verra humble apartment, and I learned to cook in the fireplace there."

He sank into the chair and hooked an ankle over his knee, the most relaxed she'd seen him. As if he sat in a fine drawing room in Edinburgh rather than this bucolic cottage, he said, "So, Miss Emeline LeClair of Edinburgh. Tell me about yerself."

Surprised, she puzzled her eyebrows as she claimed a chair too. Rarely did anyone ask about her. In fact, she couldn't recall the last time. She was invisible. Unimportant. Unremarkable.

She lifted a shoulder. "There's no' much to tell. My life has been one of restriction and restraint." Such is the case when one is poor, unwanted, and a disgrace. "I assure ye, there's nothin' excitin' or entertainin' about any of it."

"Humor me just the same, lass." A distinct twinkle sparked in those dove-gray eyes.

Eyes a woman could lose herself in. She quite liked this charming aspect of Liam Mackay.

"Start with how old ye are," he encouraged with a ghost of a smile.

"I was four and twenty on my birthday in October." She fiddled with the cuff of her gown, slightly uncomfortable confiding in him. She was on the shelf by any standard—a confirmed spinster through the misfortune of her birth.

Overlooked. Disregarded. Ignored. One did learn to exist as a shadow.

"What else?" He gave her an encouraging nod, flexing his eyes the merest bit, indicating that she should go on.

She couldn't help but respond to his genial demeanor. Whatever had sent him hightailing away earlier like a pack of rabid wolves nipped his bum must've passed. This amiable scamp was impossible to resist. Still, revealing she was a bastard humiliated her.

Most people judged her harshly when that unfortunate fact became known. As if she'd had anything to do with the circumstances of her birth. People were, in her opinion, rather horrid most of the time.

Always judging by a vacillating set of dubious standards they compiled and altered as they saw fit.

When she remained silent, he tilted his mouth into a wickedly suggestive smile and waggled his eyebrows. "Emeline," he coaxed, in his sexy rumble.

She swallowed hard and looked away. *Lord above.* How disconcerting was the ease with which she could topple into that seductive curve and enticing timbre.

Never before had a man inflamed such a maelstrom of emotion within her. Just the proximity of his virile presence sent her into a dither. With some effort, she dragged her focus away from his too-enticing presence and gathered her errant thoughts.

"My mother died in childbirth, and Aunt Jeneva raised me," she said. "She's the only family I've ever kent. Although, as I told ye, I have distant cousins in France."

He'd tamed his hair into a queue, and she decided she rather liked the few silver hairs glinting throughout. They made him look dignified and slightly mysterious.

She traced a groove on the tale with her forefinger. "Accordin' to my aunt, my grandfather was a disgraced French comte. I've nae way of kentin' if that's the truth or no'. I doubt she'd fabricate the story, however. She was a very religious woman, and I've never kent her to lie."

"And yer father?" He helped himself to another slice of bread.

A man of his size likely ate much more than she'd prepared for breakfast. She'd have to remember that. "I'm illegitimate."

The heat of a furious blush tinged her cheekbones, and she dropped her regard to her lap for a fraction. When she dared meet Liam's eyes, the expected censure and judgment wasn't there.

Instead, his head slanted, curiosity and an intense assessment shone in his pewter eyes. No doubt, he tried to absorb what she'd told him. As an unassuming spinster and illegitimate granddaughter of a French comte, what possible reason could there be for anyone to want her dead?

"Would ye like to go for a walk, Emeline? The day is quite lovely."

At the abrupt change of subject, she cast Liam a disconcerted look before dashing a glance to the vibrant blue sky beyond the window's soiled glass. "Aye. I am feelin' the need to stretch my legs and take some air."

As he efficiently banked the fire, she collected her cloak and draped it across her shoulders.

"There's quite a picturesque view of a glen a short distance away." He held the door open and waited for her to pass through. His body's heat and unique scent beckoned to her as she slipped by. "I also spotted blackberry bushes. If ye're inclined, later we can pick a bowl to eat with supper."

Why, he almost sounded like a beau trying to impress her. Of course, he wasn't, and she'd be an utter idiot to read more into his friendly gestures than he'd intended.

Allowing her first truly unfettered grin in his presence, she nodded. She did try not to appear too eager. And failed miserably. "I adore blackberries, though eatin' them was a rarity in Edinburgh."

She preceded him from the cottage, too aware of Liam directly behind her. Never before had a man's company so discomfited her. As she had since yesterday, Emeline admonished herself to remember that the strain of their meeting and everything that had occurred since had stirred her senses into acuteness.

Because, quite naturally, having looked death straight in the eye and miraculously walking away had discomposed her. A great deal. The close call had left her rattled and off-kilter. Surely that must be the reason. For, in truth, she had no idea what to do if something else went on here.

He was a hardened warrior. A wounded man. And gloriously unlike any male she'd encountered previously.

While he'd been outside attending to the hares, she'd decided to treat him as she would any casual acquaintance.

Polite. Distant. Reserved.

Only, her deuced pulse and heart, not to mention every inch of skin, responded in such a foreign way when in his proximity that she was hard put not to stutter and fumble as if inebriated.

For several minutes, they walked in companionable silence. Undoubtedly, he also had much on his mind. For instance, explaining the presence of a strange woman with him when he arrived home days later than anticipated.

Spying a white-breasted, gray-green bird with a black collar perched atop a pine branch, she pointed. "What type of bird is that?"

Liam squinted, looking to where she indicated. "'Tis a crested tit, also called a crestie."

"'Tis so pretty. Is that whose song I've been hearin'?" She put a hand to her forehead to shade her eyes and peered up at the small bird.

"Probably," he agreed amiably. "They're generally quite shy but abundant in this area."

Closing her eyes, a fleeting smile curving her mouth, Emeline breathed deeply. "It smells wonderful here. Clean and invigoratin'. I thought the same while I was visitin' Berget. I dinna miss the city's stench and cloyin' odors. Edinburgh is so verra crowded, and it smells awful."

"Och, that's true enough." He helped her over a fallen tree. "Life in the Highlands is no' easy, but her people are hearty and unwillin' to exchange this life for anythin' else."

His wife hadn't been. But then again, she'd been a Sassenach. Maybe she'd never been able to adjust to her new home or the Highlander she'd wed. Some might consider Liam gruff and intimidating, but from the moment Emeline had met him, he'd been considerate, if not entirely affable.

A few minutes later, they reached the opening he'd spoken of at the edge of the woods. The tall expanse of trees parted onto a vast, sublime expanse. Purple and pink heather yet colored the lush emerald hillsides, but the storm's damage was evident as well. As far as she could see, branches had snapped, and many trees had toppled. Where the river had previously rambled sedately on its tumbling journey to the ocean, yesterday's torrent had ravaged the banks, leaving mud and debris in its wake.

Her attention focused on the destruction, Emeline scrutinized the scene before her.

Liam hadn't exaggerated the devastation, and it was obvious why they couldn't leave yet. She pressed her palms to her belly to quiet the ponies prancing there. They might very well be stranded longer than three days. Smothering the wave of apprehension cresting in her stomach, she asked, "Where's yer home from here?"

"There. Beyond that hill." He turned slightly and extended his forefinger due west.

She glanced at him, uncertain and hesitant. "Liam?'

He slanted an eyebrow questioningly.

She wet her lower lip again and, losing her nerve, stared out over the horizon once more. "Would ye...? What I mean is... I've been thinkin' while ye were outside..."

Good God. She couldn't form a simple sentence.

Lips pursed, she blew out a frustrated breath. Squaring her shoulders, she met his gaze straight on. "I wanted to ask if ye'd consider accompanyin' me to Edinburgh."

A hawkish, raven eyebrow rose another inch, his features turning as flinty and unyielding as his eyes. "Why?"

The clipped word held more than inquiry.

Suspicion and doubt? Distrust, for certain. And if she wasn't mistaken—and she was fairly certain she wasn't—accusation too.

He was a man who didn't trust easily. But then, his wife had given him good reason not to. Still, wasn't it obvious why? He'd make her spell the reason out in spades?

She planted her hands on her hip, giving into her vexation. "Well, I canna verra well go by myself, now can I? It would be too dangerous to traipse about alone, and I ken nae other man I can ask." Oddly chagrined, a rueful smile bent her mouth as she sliced him a side-eyed look. "I truly dinna have many friends and nae male acquaintances at all."

A look of pity temporarily softened his countenance.

How she loathed those solicitous glances.

She knew what people thought. Had heard the whispers behind her back at the few functions she was invited to and permitted to attend.

By-blow. Born on the wrong side of the blanket. Child born without benefit of clergy. Illegitimate granddaughter to a count. Bastard.

"I'm also convinced that if there's anythin' that will reveal who the men were who tried to kill me or who might've hired them, I'll find it amongst my aunt's things in Edinburgh," she offered, taking care to soften her tone while not sounding pleading.

"I'll consider it, Emeline."

Hope swelled.

"But no' until after I've seen to my responsibilities at home," he said.

And just as swiftly that hope was dashed to shards upon the rocks of disappointment.

He dipped her a swift, indiscernible look before he, too, stared out over the valley. His profile chiseled angles and planes, his granite-like jaw flexed periodically. As if he fought an internal battle. "It may be a few weeks. Which, actually, could work to yer benefit if whoever hired those curs believes the assassins were successful."

She didn't see how that was the case and wanted to argue that the sooner she returned to Edinburgh and searched the apartments and shop, the sooner she might find a clue.

Did he have any idea how unnerving it was to know someone wanted her dead? *Unnerving?* No, downright terrifying.

Nonetheless, the unflinching resolution in his stance and

the knowledge that she'd already incommoded him signifi-cantly had her pasting a false, acquiescent smile on her face.

"I understand, Liam. If it werena for me, ye'd be home already. I do wonder, however, how ye will explain my pres-ence to yer family?"

"How, indeed?" His gravity dissolving, he chuckled and shook his head. "A wee waif with nae luggage or a chaperone."

Irritation welled behind her breastbone, and she bristled.

This wasn't funny. Nothing about this situation was humorous.

"I'm hardly wee, nor am I a waif. Waifs, by their very defi-nition, are strays, without a home or friends." Damn, he was right. She felt even worse.

He must've sensed her vexation, for he took her hand in his and gave it a gentle squeeze. His large palm completely engulfed hers. "I think the truth is best. Yer coach was swept away durin' a flash flood, and I saved ye. Ye're the only survivor."

"What happens if they question where we've been since the flood?" There was no easy way around that obstacle. A single day might be explained away, but several days? No, that proved much more complicated.

"Nae one needs to ken when the flood occurred. Nor does anyone need to ken how long we've been alone together." Raven eyebrows crashing together and his mouth sliding into a grim ribbon, his countenance grew fierce as he rasped, "Ye should ken, it willna make any difference if anyone does find out. I willna be playin' the gallant and proposin', Em."

Em?

Proposin'?

Why, the arrogant, conceited, puffed-up boor.

His voice as unyielding and cold as steel, he forged onward. "Dinna mistake my aid as somethin' more than it is or expect anythin' else from me. Ye're bonnie as a rose in the mornin' sun, and yer luscious shape would make the goddess of love jealous. But by God, I never mean to be duped into marriage again. Do ye understand?"

Acerbic contempt laced his words, and he spoke with such vehemence that she recoiled as if struck. He had delivered a verbal blow. Fierce and below the belt, the overbearing bounder. Taking an involuntary step backward, Emeline glared as her wrath burst into a wild, unrestrained conflagration.

"I am no' a simpleton. I understand *perfectly*, Baron. But ye should ken that I'm no' so desperate or lackin' in self-worth that such a despicable thought would've ever crossed my mind until ye mentioned it just now." She looked him up and down, from his impossibly untamed mane to his too-big feet, permitting her upper lip to curl the merest bit as her focus came to rest on his face. "No' all women are connivin' vipers, and ye've nae right to be insultin'."

Astonishment, or perhaps bewilderment, flashed across the planes of his guarded features. "Em...? I..." Liam abruptly snapped his mouth shut.

What? No barbed rejoinders now that he'd spelled his intent out in terms a deaf and dumb lackwit could understand?

Reputation shredded or not, there'd be no marriage proposal for her. Which was just as well since no power on earth—or in heaven either, for that matter—would've induced her to marry a cantankerous barbarian like him.

They were strangers thrust together by a series of unfortunate events. Nothing more. She expected nothing from him and, most assuredly, he should anticipate the same from her.

"My name is *Emeline,* no' Em," she replied, with enough starch and frost Aunt Jeneva would've applauded. Eyebrows arched haughtily, she touched her chin. "Do ye really think every woman finds ye so irresistibly desirable they'd welcome such an absurd offer if ye made it? Ye can rest easy on that account. I'd never accept. *Never.*"

SIX

Four excruciatingly long days trudged past, and Emeline and Liam settled into a loose routine. Each morning, he hunted while she bathed and prepared breakfast. When he returned, they'd share their simple meal. Afterward, he'd clean his kill, muck out Deri's lean-to, and chop wood. She straightened the cabin, washed the dishes and the few towels and cloths, and put bread on to rise.

He hadn't deserved it after his callous behavior, but she'd made an apple pie and a berry tart too. Not a bite of either treat remained. The man ate as if he were hollow to his toes, and more than once she suspected he'd been hungry despite her efforts to prepare enough food. Accustomed to cooking for two slight women with small appetites, she'd been hard-pressed to determine how much food to prepare.

In addition to hares, he'd harvested three grouse and had caught several fish yesterday and today. A less than understated way of letting her know to cook more. She'd obliged without complaint, for it wasn't her nature to be churlish or hold a grudge for his oafish behavior that first day.

Those that held on to rancor and resentment only hurt themselves. They became bitter and toxic to be around.

In the afternoon, they shared another meal, and then she'd go for a walk while he chopped *more* wood.

How much confounded firewood did they need?

And must he perform the task shirtless? Displaying his delicious, sun-kissed sculpted back, chest, and arms that no mere mortal women could possibly ignore or cease to surreptitiously ogle? Or yearn to caress that glistening, muscled form?

Torture. That was what it was. Sheer torture. If Emeline didn't know better, she'd swear he did so to deliberately put her off her stride.

Twice, she'd returned from a lengthy outing to come upon him glistening with sweat, muscles rippling in an animalist grace as he swung the ax. She'd turned on her heels and made directly for the creek to cool her toes. And the rest of her, though she only waded to her knees.

Though the brook ran high, it had a wide shoreline and hadn't flooded as the river had.

Later, while she prepared dinner, he'd take Deri for a ride and scout the terrain to determine if it was safe for them to leave on the morrow. Each time, Liam returned perceptibly disappointed that they must wait another day to depart.

She refused to examine why his disappointment piqued her. It wasn't as if she relished remaining here. Nevertheless, his eagerness to leave stung.

After dinner, he took himself off to bathe in the cold brook. Emeline studiously read *Paradise Lost* and tried, unsuccessfully for the most part, not to think of the naked man behind the cottage. She either read this tediously long and rather depressing poem by Milton or *The Essays* by Sir Francis Bacon.

Neither book was particularly entertaining or uplifting.

Most assuredly, Liam and his friends hadn't spent their leisure reading. Honestly, she suspected the only reason the books were here was that one of them had wanted to rid their library of the works.

When Liam returned from his evening ablutions, he sharpened his sword and dirk. True to his word, he hadn't laid a hand on her and had treated her with utmost respect and courtesy since his outburst. Impossible as it seemed, he'd reinforced the already impermeable walls he'd erected.

Nevertheless, she often caught him watching her, his smoky-gray eyes inscrutable slits. She couldn't count the number of times *she* covertly studied the bewildering man as well. It had been insulting and humiliating beyond endurance when he'd growled that he'd not be making an honest woman of her. As if she anticipated any such thing or had in any way hinted that she did.

"Bonnie as a rose in the morn and a shape to make a goddess jealous" indeed.

She pressed cool hands to heated cheeks, admonishing her capering pulse and vivid imagination to behave themselves. Eyes and attention trained upon the yellowed page, she worried her lower lip.

So forcible within my heart I feel
The bond of nature draw me to my own,
My own in thee, for what thou art is mine;
Our state cannot be severed, we are one,
One flesh; to lose thee were to lose myself.

Flames licked her cheeks once more. *Good heavens.* Was she destined to burn cherry-red all evening?

Cheery whistling interrupted her attempt to immerse herself in the poem. Head tilted, she raised her attention from the tome. *Did Liam whistle?* Or...did someone else approach the cottage?

Alarm flitted through her and, once she'd grabbed the fire poker, she crept to the window. The sun hung low on the horizon. Faint streaks of purple and pink pastels feathered the dusky blue sky between the tree branches.

Liam's mane of wet ebony hair bounced upon his shoulders as he marched up the slight incline. *Whistling.* Relief swept her. She hadn't known exactly what she'd do if someone else besides him had been outside.

She adored his hair, and she itched to thread her fingers through its silky lengths. She'd never seen a man with more magnificent hair. Many of the females frequenting Aunt Jeneva's shop would've gnashed their teeth for locks half so lovely. The shiny tresses were wasted on a man.

His beard intrigued too. Mostly because of what it hid.

Liam fairly beamed as he burst into the cottage. So excited was he, she wouldn't have been surprised if he'd kicked his heels together. "Lass, we leave on the morrow."

Emeline ought to have been overjoyed, but dismay better described the emotion tightening her chest. Having him nearby day and night had taxed her nerves and her reserves to no end. Yet, the truth was, once they left this cottage and she accompanied him to his home, this camaraderie would end. That knowledge reinforced her loneliness and apprehension.

He knew what awaited him. Knew what to expect. Emeline, however, had no idea what her future held.

And always—*always*— lurking ominously in the shadows was the knowledge that someone wanted her dead. Someone desperate or determined enough to go to the extremes of locating her while she was on holiday in the Highlands and replacing the drivers with hired cutthroats.

Until that matter was solved, she'd never be at ease. Her gut instincts told her she couldn't solve the mystery without help. And she didn't even need the fingers of one hand to count the number of people she could impose upon to assist her.

However, Liam's grin proved contagious, and she smiled in return. All the while, making certain her gaze didn't stray to the tempting dark hair peeking from the opening of his unlaced shirt.

Upon spying the poker in her white-knuckled grip, he elevated a raven eyebrow. "Did ye mean to clobber me with that or run me through?"

"I dinna ken who approached." Self-conscious and feeling ridiculous, she returned the poker to the holder on the hearth.

Still grinning, he held up a good-sized kettle filled with water. "I found this in the lean-to's loft. I thought ye could wash yer hair tonight if ye wanted to," he said, striding to the fireplace and hanging the pot on the hook.

Must he be so blasted giddy that they were finally leaving? And was her appearance so hideous that he wanted to make sure she was presentable when they arrived tomorrow? Nonetheless, making a good impression couldn't hurt, and that was better accomplished with a well-scrubbed scalp.

"That would be wonderful. Thank ye for suggestin' it." Despite the uncharacteristic peevishness that had swept her, her response was sincere. The offer was simply too welcome to resist. It had been over a week since she washed the mass tied at her nape.

He waved toward the door. "I thought we could put a chair outside, and ye could lean back. Then I can help wet it and wash it."

She gawked as if a trow had parted his beard, poked its ugly head out, winked, and brazenly waved. God save her, but the suggestion was far too intimate. Far too tempting. If he touched her—

"Ye dinna have to help me," she hastily declined. "I'm accustomed to washin' my hair myself."

He cupped his nape and gave her a boyish half-grin. "Aye, but I'll wager ye're no' accustomed to doin' so from a kettle outdoors."

And that was why, fifteen minutes later, she stood uncertainly outside the cottage.

The evening had turned cool but not unpleasantly so.

Deri whickered for his master and shifted his feet.

"Ye're a glutton for attention, lad," Liam called to the horse. "There's a lass requirin' my consideration at present."

Deri snorted and rolled his big brown eyes as if to say, *Just wait until ye wish to ride me again.*

"Have a seat, lass." Patting the chair back, Liam pulled a face. "I dinna think I can manage with ye standin'."

He assuredly could too. He stood a foot taller than she.

"I told ye, ye dinna have to do this." Having already untied the strip of cloth holding her hair back, Emeline obediently, if somewhat reluctantly, plopped onto the chair as he'd indicated. Acutely aware of the handsome man who'd soon be touching her hair, she swallowed around the constriction in her throat.

She had nothing to be nervous about, Emeline strongly admonished herself. Nevertheless, there was something so very intimate about allowing him to wash her hair. It unnerved and thrilled at the same time. She clasped the linen cloth about her shoulders tighter, as much for something to do with her hands as from nerves stretched taut as bowstrings.

"I've never washed a woman's hair before."

All the more reason for him not to wash hers.

Instead, she softly said, "No' even yer wife's?"

His low chuckle surprised her. She'd expected anger at the mention of his wife. "Nae, Kristin preferred her lady's maid perform the task."

So her name had been Kristin.

What kind of woman had she been?

From the little Liam had shared, not a very admirable one.

Emeline knew she'd been English, of course, and she and Liam had two children together. His wife hadn't liked the Highlands, and his caustic remark about being duped gave Emeline reason to wonder if the union had been entirely by choice.

Moving behind the chair, he carefully lifted her long hair over the back. He ran his hands down the tresses a few times before gathering the mass together.

"Let me ken if I accidentally pull yer hair. Ye've quite a lot." He cleared his throat, and she ducked her chin, smiling.

Had he bitten off more than he could chew?

Did he now regret his gallant offer? Hadn't he said he *wasn't* a gallant?

What else did one call a man who went out of his way to treat and assist a woman?

"I shall," she murmured. "I confess, this is rather a treat. I've never had a lady's maid before."

He poured the first bowls of warm water over her hair, running his big hand down the strands. Two more scoops followed. The distinct aroma of Castile soap wafted past her nostrils. After drawing the bar over her hair from scalp to the ends several times, he added a bit more water and worked the soap into a frothy lather.

She'd expected he'd use the same soft soap in the jar she'd been using for bathing. This must be his personal bar. He'd used it all over his body. And though it shouldn't have, the thought sent another burst of excitement pelting along her nerves.

Unable to resist relaxing as he gently rubbed her scalp and washed her hair, Emeline closed her eyes. Now she understood why fancy ladies might enjoy this regularly. When she'd washed her hair at home, it had been a quick process.

Well, as quick as it could be with hair hanging to her waist.

"How does that feel?" Liam's voice held a slightly husky note.

She mustered a lazy, closed-mouth ghost of a smile. "I fear, I could get quite accustomed to this pampering." Her bones felt the consistency of warm wax and her eyelids weighted by bricks.

"Ye've beautiful hair," he said, scarcely above a whisper—almost as if he unwillingly spoke his thoughts aloud. "The color's unusual. No' quite auburn and no' quite sable."

His was black as a moonless, starless night. Except for the silver. Those were the stars glittering in the midnight sky.

She chuckled and, arching her neck, opened her eyes, peering backward at him. "Nae one's ever described my hair that way. I simply call it dark brown, as did my aunt." She scrunched her nose. "Although, now that I think on it, I believe she mentioned an auburn-haired female somewhere in the family tree."

"Nae, nothin' so common as dark brown for ye, Emeline." His voice sounded a soft caress as his fingers stilled. "Chestnut. Bronze. Treacle. Whisky."

"*Whisky*? I'm no' sure that's a compliment, Liam." She chuckled, slightly shaking her head.

"If ye ken how much I enjoy whisky, ye'd have nae doubt, *leannan*," he replied in that spine-caressing deep brogue.

Such an innocent comment shouldn't have sent thrills rippling from breast to knees, but—God save her—it did. She was reading too much into his actions and words. That was what inexperience wrought. He was a man of the world and, no doubt, hadn't a second thought about his rascally speech.

"Och, Emeline. Close yer eyes and dinna move. A bit of soap is drippin' down yer forehead." A moment later, he bent closer, so near she smelled the Castilian soap scenting his still-damp hair. He swiped the soap away, and, at his touch, a tremor rippled through her.

She might blame it on the cooling evening, but she knew it for what it was.

Desire. For Liam.

"I'm goin' to rinse now," he said, a queer inflection in his tone.

Did he know? Was she so transparent?

"Keep yer eyes closed," he said.

As if she dared open them and have him read in her gaze what she'd been hiding since they'd first met. He might be an untamed Scot with no use for women—*och, only one use*—but from the instant he'd plopped her on Deri, her body had been much too aware of him.

Several more tepid bowls of water flowed over her head and hair. With each, Liam combed his thick fingers from her scalp to the ends of the tresses. She'd never been more relaxed or felt more indulged in her entire life. There was something very nice about having one's hair washed. That she couldn't deny, particularly by a startlingly virile man.

After gathering her sopping wet hair and twisting it into a rope, he wrung the water out. He smoothed his big palms from her forehead, over the back of her head, and then raked his fingers through her long tresses several times.

Now that the sun had sunk below the horizon, a slight breeze had kicked up. The evening had grown chilly, and she shivered.

"Let's get ye inside before the fire, and get yer hair dry." He patted her shoulder, his voice neutral once more. "We dinna need ye catchin' a chill."

Aye, because that would delay our departure.

SEVEN

With legs made of jelly and a distinct reluctance to move, Emeline sighed. She took the towel from around her shoulders and wrapped her hair. Summoning her nerve, she bent her lips upward shyly and faced him. "Thank ye, Liam."

To her utter astonishment and a delighted skip of her heart, he dipped into a courtier's bow. "It was my pleasure, my lady. Now inside with ye. I'll bring the chair."

"Aye, sir." Giving him another radiant smile over her shoulder, she dutifully filed into the cottage.

He might be reluctant to admit it, but no man washed a woman's hair if he didn't feel something for her. She wasn't sure what or where it might lead, but happiness like warm molasses burbled behind her ribs.

Setting her teeth against the waves of shudders rippling through her, she squatted and added two logs to the fading fire. She prodded the coals until flames snapped and crackled, sending heat radiating outward into the room, before removing the linen from her hair.

Shaking the long tresses down her spine, she hauled a chair

before the hearth. She'd positioned herself far enough away so that she'd not overheat but close enough her hair would dry when Liam entered. He shut and bolted the door, then set the kettle in the corner.

Wordlessly, he carried the other chair to where she sat. "Em, stand up for a minute."

Giving him a curious look, and declining to remind him again that her name wasn't Em, she stood.

He positioned her chair just so, and once he'd collected a blanket from her bed and draped it across the back of her chair, situated himself beside her. "Now, ye can sit."

Slowly lowering herself, she gave him another inquisitive glance. "What are ye about?"

"Ye can rest yer head against the chair's back without risk of a crick in yer neck. I should've thought of that outside." With a big palm to her shoulder, he eased her backward. "I'm sorry I dinna have a comb or brush." He gave her another one of his charming, heart-stuttering grins. "But I wasna expectin' to entertain a lady."

The way he said *entertain a lady* sent a secret thrill through her. To wrangle her wayward musings and bring her leaping pulse under control, she asked, "So conditions are safe for us to travel tomorrow then?"

"Aye."

He combed his fingers through her hair, and she stifled a groan. This was pure heaven. Who knew having someone attend to her hair could be so sensual? So evocative? So addictive?

"I'd like to leave at dawn. We'll take it slow, but I still think we will reach Eytone Hall by midafternoon." Another slow drag of those long fingers to her hair, gently tugging at her scalp, and a zip of pleasure skittered down her spine.

How was she to sit behind him for hours and hours, her arms around his solid torso, and her breasts brushing his muscle-ridden back and maintain her poise? She didn't suppose he'd let her walk.

Don't be ridiculous. Emeline bit her lip. Of course not. His home was too far.

She'd have to clench her teeth and think of unpleasant things: *Liver. Mushrooms. Beets.*

That wasn't working at all.

Something darker and more dire then: *What am I goin' to do now that Aunt Jeneva is gone? Who wants me dead?*

The latter two sobering thoughts didn't produce the desired results either.

How could they when Liam still touched her?

"I dinna ken if the usual roads and pathways are accessible. So we may have to take alternate routes." Again and again and again, he spread his fingers through her hair, each a hypnotic caress that had her all but melting on the chair.

Did the nearness affect him too, or was a man of the world such as he immune to such provocations?

He nudged her shoulder. "Em, have ye fallen asleep?"

"Emeline," she murmured drowsily, too comfortable to bother opening her eyes. "We have bread left and some of the rabbit meat too. I'll wrap the food in the mornin'."

"Aye, and I've already filled my canteen." Yes, his voice held a distinct rasp. As if he, too, struggled to control this uncontrollable desire sparking between them.

"Liam?"

"Aye?"

"What happened to yer face?" The thought became spoken words before she realized they'd slipped from her lips. Curse her curiosity and loose tongue.

His hands calmed in her hair, and he remained perfectly still and silent for so long that she assumed she'd offended him. Well, of course, she had with her blatant snooping. *Dolt.*

"I beg your pardon. I oughtna have asked somethin' so personal. Forgive me." Thank God she'd closed her eyes. She couldn't bear to see his scorn directed at her.

To her astonishment, he began rubbing her scalp again.

"My wife attacked me. She...she often imbibed too liberally in spirits and had a fierce temper when she did." His voice rumbled low and controlled as if speaking of the incident strained his resolve. "One afternoon, already deep in her cups, she took our daughter for a walk. In her drunken state, Kristin wasna as attentive as she should've been, and Mareona wandered to the lake. She adored the ducks, ye see."

Had his children looked like him?

They'd been quite young at the time of their deaths. Emeline wasn't sure she would ever have been able to recover from such a horrific loss. It would have broken her spirit. She supposed after something so life-altering, a person lived a new reality. What had been could never be again.

He changed the angle of his fingers until he was rubbing slow circles at her temples.

A moan of pure bliss formed in her throat, but she swallowed it down.

"A gardener spotted the bairn toddlin' about alone too near the waters and returned her to the house. When I arrived home that evenin' and learned of the mishap, I went straightaway to Kristin's chambers."

That couldn't have been pleasant.

Emeline felt she should say something but honestly had no idea what. Anything she said would seem trite and insufficient. Her heart swelled with emotion that he would share this story with her, the telling of which obviously pained him.

"What happened, Liam?"

"I informed her that I intended to instruct my family and staff that she was nae longer permitted to be alone with our children." His fingers went still. "She became enraged and seized a letter opener—"

Emiline's horrified gasp interrupted him. *Oh my God.* She'd attacked her husband.

"Och, ye can see the results." Unlike that first day, no restrained wrath weighted his words.

However, righteous anger sent Emeline's blood boiling. His wife had been an unhinged banshee. How had he ever come to marry such an evil woman?

That question would have to wait for another time. Not only wasn't it any of her business, but Liam had waded through enough miry, unpleasant memories for one night.

She leisurely lifted her eyelids, and her gaze locked with his. Something more than firelight glittered in their arresting slate-gray depths. When his focus sank to her mouth, she could no more have stopped her tongue from darting out and moistening the lower lip than she could have halted the flash flood of a few days ago.

A torrent of a different sort flowed through her every bit as powerful as those riotous waters.

She wanted Liam to kiss her. Needed him to.

For days, she'd yearned for his firm mouth on hers, even when he'd vexed her to no end. Even though he'd made it perfectly clear that while he'd rescued her, he offered her nothing more. Owed her nothing more.

And he didn't—not a thing.

"Em?" His question rang with an unspoken suggestion.

"Emeline," she countered, needing the control that requiring him to call her by her given name and not a pet name afforded her.

His gravelly whisper came a mere exciting inch from her mouth.

"Obstinate lass." His words rang as an endearment rather than a scold.

"Pig-headed boor," she countered. Most definitely an endearment.

With a throaty groan, he clasped one big hand behind her head and cupped her chin with the other. The first brush of his lips was light. Fleeting. The merest wisp of a butterfly's wing. A tantalizing tease. A heady promise, leaving her wanting more. More. *More.*

"Liam?"

Good God and all the angels. Was that husky purr her voice? She looped her arms around his neck, drawing him near, telling him with her body what she was too bashful to say with words. Curling her fingers into his magnificent hair, she clung to him.

He crushed her to his hard body, his mouth swooping down upon hers in a scorching assault. She gasped in excitement and surprise. She hadn't expected the kiss to be so powerful. All-consuming. So blissfully wonderful.

His beard was surprisingly soft, the gentle friction adding to her arousal.

At his gentle prodding, she opened her mouth, eager to get

closer. To taste more of him. Their breaths and tongues tangled, a heated, ravenous frenzy. Without lifting his mouth from hers, he drew her upward and scooped her into his arms. In four long strides, he reached her bed and reverently laid her upon the insufficient mattress.

This was madness. Utter recklessness. Emeline's sensible self screamed for her to put an end to the insanity. But the lonely, ignored, overlooked, and disregarded four and twenty-year-old sensual woman thrilled that such a prime specimen of manhood should find her desirable. *Her!*

When he stretched out beside her—all hewn sinew and hard rippling muscles—and cradled her tenderly against him, she whimpered tremulously, "Liam?"

He tore his mouth from hers and trailed hot, wet kisses over her jaw and neck before gently nipping the juncture where her throat met her collarbone.

She started and gasped at the instant jolt of burning desire spearing her. *More.* She wanted more. More of this. More of him.

She whimpered again, running her hands up and down his spine, relishing his sinewy hardness and the hunger he stirred. Never had she dreamed she could feel this way. As if every pore was alive and molten lava flowed through her veins. Hunger and desire and passion overwhelmed her and, instinctively, she knew only he could relieve this sizzling need.

She wriggled beneath him, arching her hips and curving into his corded muscles, silently pleading for more. *More.*

A seductive chuckle, melodious and bone-melting, reverberated in his chest. He lowered his head to the expanse of flesh visible above her bodice while raising her skirt and trailing his callused fingertips up her trembling thigh.

"Ye're a siren, Em. A temptation I canna resist, God help me. Ye've completely bewitched me, *jo*."

A blend of resignation and self-castigation weighted his tone, making Emeline go perfectly still.

He sounded tortured. As if desiring Emeline was a horrid, unpardonable sin. Something *he* didn't want, but his virile, healthy body craved. She could appreciate the truth of that.

A rigid lump pushed insistently into her abdomen. Oh, yes. Liam wanted her physically. Ached for her every bit as much as she hungered for him, but he loathed himself for the weakness. Loathed the desire he felt for her.

And she would despise herself, as well, if she gave herself to a man who'd end up hating himself for taking her innocence. If it weren't so heartrendingly pathetic, she'd laugh at the ludicrousness.

Because she deserved better. Because he deserved better. For both of their sakes, she did what must be done.

"Liam. Please stop." Bracing her hands upon his chest, she turned her face away. "Stop."

He went utterly still, his mouth pressed to her peaked breast through her gown. "Em...?"

"We canna do this," she forced out through swollen lips and the throbbing tightness in her throat. "Ye ken I'm right, Liam. Ye'd despise yerself afterward, and I willna let ye do somethin' ye'd regret. Somethin' that canna be undone."

Something she longed for with every pore in her body, though it meant certain ruination.

And even though wisdom decreed she ought to regret offering herself to him, she didn't. Couldn't. Not a jot of it. She'd have let him have his way and enjoyed every blissful moment if she wasn't absolutely positive remorse would consume him later.

"Och, hell." With a half-groan, half-sigh, he yanked her skirt over her thighs. When he stiffly edged away, she almost cried out at the sense of bereftness. Almost tossed her conscience to the wind, just to have him in her arms once more.

Shoulders hunched, his elbows on his knees, he sat on the edge of the bed and plowed a hand through his hair. "Christ on the cross, forgive me, lass. I dinna ken what came over me. I vowed I wouldna touch ye, and I broke that oath."

She laid her palm on his back, wincing as he stiffened, and her heart burgeoned with an unbearable ache. "I'm glad my first kiss was with ye, Liam."

Probably her only kiss. The only time her breasts would be kissed and caressed. Biting tears formed behind her eyelids.

Something that sounded like a hiss exploded past his lips. "Jesus."

"I'll always treasure this experience and the time we've had together here." She swallowed against the ridiculous lump forming in her throat and the tears blurring her vision. She would not cry. It was too late for recriminations or regret.

Heaving a great sigh, he angled to his feet.

A wounded man. A decent man. A man who so warranted happiness.

Eyebrows furrowed, one powerful forearm braced against the bunk above hers, he gazed at her with those indecipherable eyes. Eyes darkened to charcoal with passion that yet simmered there, he scrutinized her face, as if memorizing each imperfect feature.

Oh, how she wanted to smooth the creases of recrimination from his forehead. Soothe the ache in his spirit. To help him heal and live again.

"Ye're a most remarkable woman, Emeline LeClaire. Ye merit much better than a broken man like me."

Nae, I dinna. I want ye. And only ye.

"This willna happen again." It was a solemn vow, and her heart fragmented at the finality of his harshly muttered words. He turned and, after seizing the blankets off his bunk, slammed from the cottage.

At last, the tears that had threatened surged over the rims of her eyes and cascaded down her face. Pulling the pillow to her chest, she buried her face in the lumpy mass.

What have I done?

Foolish, foolish, stupid, gullible girl.

How could I have fallen in love with a man who can never, ever love me?

EIGHT

Nearly twenty hours later, Liam placed a tender kiss on Emeline's forehead before reluctantly giving her a slight shake to awaken her. "Emeline, we're here."

This magnificent woman would've given herself to him last night. She'd put a stop to their passion. Not because she didn't want to go on, but because she'd come to know him so well in such a short time that she knew he'd despise himself for losing control.

Since he'd stormed from the cottage and spent the night in the lean-to, she'd been unusually silent and distant.

Wasn't that what he'd wanted?

He'd believed it was until he'd tossed and turned all night, visions of her moist mouth, rucked nipple, and impossibly long legs taunting him.

Fine. He wanted her. He was young and healthy. She had a body that begged to be loved. He'd simply responded to an animalistic urge.

Liar.

Perchance if he kept telling himself that falsehood, he'd actually come to believe it.

He raked his gaze over her exquisite features, still relaxed in sleep. Her thick lashes fanned across her flushed cheeks dotted with adorable cinnamon-colored freckles. She breathed through her parted lips, dewy and tempting even as she slept.

It wasn't just her beauty that attracted him. She was a complex, intelligent woman. A woman who put others before herself, and if he'd met her in a different time and place, there might've been room in his heart and life for her.

But since Kristin...

"Emeline." He jostled her again. She'd been as difficult to awaken in the cottage too. He'd never known a woman to sleep so deeply. "We've arrived, and my kin awaits us, lass."

At least he expected they would descend upon him when they arrived. Ten minutes ago, a laborer had dropped his hoe and torn across the field toward the great house. No doubt, on Mother's orders to bring word the moment Liam was sighted.

"Do ye want my family and servants to see ye splayed across my lap? For certain, they'll get the wrong impression. Perhaps assume we're lovers," he said, unable to keep the teasing note from his voice.

Emeline's eyelids flew open at that pronouncement. Treacle-brown eyes sparking with embarrassment and annoyance, she straightened so abruptly that she knocked his chin with her head.

"Ouch." He rubbed the battered flesh, enjoying the rosy glow on her cheeks.

"Why didna ye say so the first time, ye clot head?" At once, she set to smoothing her hair. The ribbon containing the silky mass had been lost during the ride.

Despite her irritation, he chuckled. She was adorable when she went all prickly.

By the time they rounded the last curve of the long drive to Eytone Hall, she sat before him prim as a ninety-year-old virgin nun, eyes averted and posture demure.

He leaned forward until his lips brushed the back of her head. "Relax. They'll no' pounce."

"Hmph." She fairly trembled with trepidation. Squaring her shoulders, she gasped as Eytone Hall came into view, it's weathered buff-colored exterior and rows of mullioned windows catching the sun's last bronze rays.

"'Tis magnificent. And huge, Liam." Wonder colored her awestruck voice.

"Aye." Pride infused him. "'Tis that."

He loved his home.

For nine generations, the MacKays had overseen these lands. The very first feudal baron had commissioned the structure standing as a grand sentinel before them now. Constructed in the classical Scottish domesticated architecture style, the stately stone manor house boasted gables, towers, and several clusters of chimney stacks.

Stifling a groan, he flexed his shoulders and straightened his spine. Hours of holding Emeline had wreaked havoc on the muscles as well as his libido. Rather than have her ride astride behind him, exposing her silky inner thighs to hours of chafing as well as the long milky-white legs to his less than chaste approval, he'd opted to seat her sideways in front of him.

The problem with that choice had been that her unforgettable, evocative scent filled his nostrils, and her lush curves had swayed against him as he held her upright. A raging erection had plagued him for miles.

Hell, if he were entirely honest with himself, he'd been in a state of half-arousal since awaking that first night and seeing the tempting shadows of her gorgeous form through that filmy shift in the muted firelight.

A niggling fear tormented him that he fought a battle with this extraordinary woman he was destined to lose.

No, he'd already lost a battle against his desire last night, but he would win the war. *He must.* Desire was his enemy. *Remember that.* If he hadn't lusted after a pampered English woman, he'd not eat, breathe, and sleep with a fractured heart every minute of his life.

But Emeline is different, the neglected, battered organ cried. He couldn't take the risk. It would destroy him.

As he reined Deri to a halt in Eytone Hall's sweeping courtyard, the manor's sturdy double doors sprang open and Kendra bolted down the steps, her unbound chestnut hair flowing behind her. "Och, Liam. We've been so verra worried."

Eyes shining and breathless, she sent Emeline a curiosity-laden glance.

Composed, pale, and regal as always, his mother appeared in the entrance.

Several others crowded into the opening, included Quinn Catherwood, Broden McGregor, and—*by God*, was that his cousin Skye Hendron? Why wasn't she in England with her parents? Gone for less than a fortnight, and visitors had invaded Liam's home in his absence.

His mother glided down the half-dozen weathered stone stairs, her expression a mixture of worry and relief.

Quinn and Skye followed on her heels.

"Liam, we expected ye days ago." Mother's focus traveled to the disheveled Emeline sitting across his lap. Not so much as an eyelash flickered, but Liam knew full well she'd taken in everything about the surprise guest from Emeline's head to her toes.

His mother's keen gaze narrowed minutely.

Bloody hell. That slight flexing meant there'd be an inquisition later. A lengthy inquisition.

Lest everyone see his state of arousal, he didn't dare dismount until he'd brought his lust under control. He motioned to Broden McGregor. "Broden, please help Miss LeClaire alight."

The cross look Kendra sliced Broden piqued Liam's interest.

From his cocky grin and the acute interest in the gaze he leveled Emeline, Broden was happy to oblige. Too handsome for his own good, he winked good-naturedly and easily lifted her from the saddle.

"Och, lass. I can imagine ye require somethin' besides grunts and groans for conversation if ye've spent any time in this bear's company." His hand remained on her elbow to steady her as she became accustomed to standing after riding for so long.

A surge of possessiveness assailed Liam, and he wanted to rip his friend's fingers from her arm. The ire did much to cool his lust.

Emeline's mouth twitched at the corners, and she slid Liam a mischievous glance from beneath her lashes.

God, she was adorable.

"He sometimes growls, snorts, and hisses too," she murmured matter-of-factly.

Add a sense of humor to her considerable charms.

Quinn and Broden guffawed, and Skye and Kendra giggled. Even Mother's mouth inched upward a degree, approval shining in her eyes.

"In case anyone cares, I'm right here and can hear ye," Liam grumbled.

"Liam, darlin', I believe that's the point." His mother's eyes twinkled. "We're no' laughin' at ye, but with ye."

Emeline wasn't.

To anyone but him, she appeared composed, even serene. But he'd come to know her well these past days, and he spied the signs of her severe nervousness. Hands clasped tightly before her. Squared shoulders. The Madonna's serene smile that didn't quite reach her wide, troubled eyes.

"My dear Miss LeClaire! What an unexpected pleasure." Kendra swooped in to take Emeline's hands in hers, forcing Broden to release her arm. "'Tis wonderful to see ye again so soon." She wrapped an arm around Emeline's waist while sending Liam another inquisitive glance.

His mother's too-perceptive gaze drifted between Liam and Emeline and traveled back to Liam again before she raised her eyebrow—her most skeptical eyebrow—a fraction.

To his immense relief, no one paid him much mind as he slid from Deri. Everyone's attention was on the woman he'd brought home.

It was his turn to summon false congeniality. "I'm sure ye're curious why I'm tardy and why Miss LeClaire is with me. I'll explain inside after the introductions." He turned to his mother. "Mother, we're both ravenous. Please ask the kitchen to prepare somethin'."

At once, his mother nodded her noble head. With carefully coiffed hair as black as his but liberally threaded with silver, she had the bearing of a great lady as well as a genuinely warm and generous heart. "Of course. Baths too, I presume?"

"Please." He bent to kiss her upturned cheek. "I'm sorry to have worried ye."

She gripped his forearm, her expression more relaxed. "Ye're home safe now. That's what counts."

Looking slightly lost, Emeline met his gaze across the short distance separating them. He canted his head, indicating she should accompany Kendra inside.

"Kendra, I'm hopin' I can impose upon ye to allow Emeline to borrow a few of yer gowns." Liam flexed his spine again. Miles of riding while wanting a woman he couldn't possess had strained his self-control mightily.

"Of course." She gave Emeline a reassuring smile, even as her winged brows dipped together in puzzlement. To her credit, his outspoken sister didn't ask the obvious question.

Nonetheless, a flush scampered across Emeline's porcelain cheeks.

Her rosy cheeks didn't escape his mother's notice, however, and her eyebrows scampered up her forehead. She wisely refrained from commenting as well. For now.

"Liam, we heard word of flash floodin' and several fatalities. I must tell ye, we were all greatly concerned when ye didna arrive home on time." Broden slapped him on the shoulder, then gave it a hard squeeze. "Glad I am to see ye safe and sound."

They'd heard of the flash flood? *Dammit.*

Liam had counted on them not being aware. The tense line of Emeline's jaw revealed her thoughts mirrored his. The account they'd agreed to tell everyone would need altering a mite.

Kendra tossed her head and rolled her eyes heavenward. "Broden, I told ye he was fine. Ye needna have come to check on him or us."

"Kendra, cease bein' churlish to our guest," Mother gently admonished. "The Penderhavens and MacKays are kent far and wide for our hospitality, and Broden dinna need an invitation to call. He's always welcome in our home."

"Aye, but some guests *outstay* their welcome." She gave Broden a pointed look, and his expression turned flinty. Since when did she snipe at him? And since when did he look like he wanted to turn her over his knee?

Eyes narrowed contemplatively, Liam considered them. For all of their protestations of dislike, they could hardly keep their eyes off each other.

A few minutes later, everyone entered Eytone Hall's floral salon. At least that was what Mother called the garish room. Decorated in shades of pinks and roses, with gewgaws galore scattered about, Liam called the damned feminine travesty an eyesore. If his mother knew the salon greatly resembled a courtesans' bordello, she'd faint dead away.

He took Emeline's elbow and, offering her a reassuring upward slant of his mouth, guided her to his mother. "Mother, may I present Miss Emeline LeClaire? Emeline, my mother, Louisa MacKay, Baroness of Penderhaven."

Emeline dipped into an elegant curtsy, a graceful smile curving her lips. "'Tis a pleasure to make yer acquaintance, my lady. Please forgive the imposition."

His mother arced her hand in the air. "Think nothin' of it, my dear. We adore havin' guests." She laughed, a light, cheerful tinkle. "Ye smell far better than the hairy mongrel Liam brought home a few weeks ago."

"Prince would be most offended to hear ye speak so ill of him. He adores ye." Liam glanced around, then frowned. "Where is he, anyway?"

"Havin' a bath in the stables. Yer Prince is noble in name only. The beast is fond of rollin' in sheep and *coo* manure, and I draw the line at animal excrement in my home." Lady Penderhaven motioned to Skye. "Miss LeClaire, this is my sister's daughter and my niece, Skye Hendron."

A kind smile swept Skye's face, and she grasped Emeline's hand. "I'm sure we'll be the greatest of friends." Though half-Scots, Skye had lived in England her entire life and acted every bit the perfect Englishwoman.

Liam bent his neck and kissed his cousin's cheek. "I'm glad to see ye, but I didna ken ye were plannin' a visit." He angled his head toward his mother inquisitively.

"'Tis an unexpected pleasure," his mother said, a hint of concern creasing the corners of her eyes.

Skye's blue eyes clouded and worry tautened her already high cheekbones. "Mama sent me north. A week ago, Papa returned to England from a visit to France and fell extremely ill within days. Mama insisted I come to Eytone Hall the same day. I didn't even have a chance to bid him farewell." She absently plucked at the lace at her elbow. "I hope 'tis nothing serious."

"As do we all," Mother agreed soberly.

Wasn't there a plague outbreak in France?

Liam would bite his tongue off before he mentioned it, however.

Her gray eyes bright with curiosity, Kendra fairly bounced on the tips of her toes. "I canna imagine how ye came to be in Liam's company. When did ye leave Killeaggian Tower? I thought Berget said ye intended an extended stay."

About as subtle as an enraged bull in the larder was his sister.

Everyone's attention shifted to Liam and Emeline, inquisitiveness etched upon their features, but each too polite to put forward the question Kendra hinted at. As the last rays of sun filtered through the windows, casting the room in a warm light, Emeline looked as if she'd swallowed rocks.

"My aunt decided she shouldna be away from her modiste shop any longer," she said by way of an explanation.

Likely, Jeneva LeClaire couldn't afford to be away longer. Clientele was only so loyal. She'd only answered why they'd left Killeaggian, however. Emeline fixed her innocent whisky-colored eyes on Liam, trusting him to modify the story they'd agreed to tell. They'd also decided to forgo her assuming a false identity since Kendra knew Emeline, and using a false name would raise questions neither were ready to answer just yet.

"I was on my way home when the thunderstorm hit—the worst I've ever encountered," he put forth, attempting to steer the conversation in a different direction.

His mother and sister nodded simultaneously.

"It sounded as if the heavens were collapsin'." Kendra gave an exaggerated shudder, her face a shade paler. She'd always hated storms, particularly thunderstorms.

Liam swept his gaze to each of the room's occupants in turn. "As ye can well imagine, it was quite dangerous with the trees fallin', lightnin' strikin', and the tremendous rainfall makin' the ground unstable. I happened across a coach as a flash flood bore down upon the occupants. I only just managed to reach Emeline and see her to higher ground before the water consumed the conveyance. Unfortunately, the drivers and her aunt perished."

All perfectly true, but only partially accurate, given the disturbing details he'd omitted.

Kendra gasped and blanched. "Och, Emeline, I'm so verra sorry." Her countenance sharpened by compassion, his spitfire of a sister blinked away genuine tears.

Broden and Quinn made appropriate sympathetic noises as well, and his mother *tsked* her commiserations. "How utterly tragic, my dear. Please accept my deepest condolences, Emeline."

"Thank ye." Fingers formed into talons, Emeline clenched the fabric of her cloak and directed her focus to the floor. Her throat worked, and Liam didn't doubt she relived those terrifying moments when the gun was pointed at her, her aunt's violent death, and how they'd barely escaped the floodwaters.

"But the storm was days ago—?" Broden ceased abruptly at the thunderous scowl Liam speared him.

Comprehension caused his mother's eyes to flex the merest bit before she cleared her throat and directed her attention to Emeline again. "My dear girl, I shall have a bath drawn for ye at once. Kendra, hurry to yer room and gather an assortment of clothin', underthin's, and nightwear for our guest."

"Liam, dinna I get an introduction?" Broden gave a cheeky grin. Not for the first time today, Liam wanted to wipe it from his face. Preferably with his fist.

He'd never felt hostility toward Broden until today, and the unwelcome sensation made bile rise hot and acrid in his throat. He curled his fingers into his palm and marshaled his composure. "I'm no' sure that's a good idea, given yer reputation."

"Nae worse than yers, my friend," Broden quipped, not the least bit put off by Liam's starchy demeanor.

"God above and all the saints too, give me patience." Kendra rolled her eyes again and snorted. "And men complain women prattle on about nothin'."

In short order, Liam introduced Emeline to Broden and Quinn.

She gave each a shy smile, and Liam wanted to punch his handsome friends in the face. He didn't like this possessiveness thrumming through him, making him think and behave rashly. Hadn't he spent years learning to control his impulses? And then this bonnie lass with her doe eyes comes along and turns everything arse over chin.

"I believe I saw ye at McCulloughs' ball in Edinburgh, Mr. McGregor," she said, tucking a strand of hair behind her ear. "Werena ye dressed as a sheik?"

"Aye, he was struttin' about like a vain peacock." Arms crossed, and her tone as dry and heated as fresh ash, Kendra cast him a sour look. "Because he mistakenly believes that *all* women will fall under his spell and jump at the opportunity to join his harem."

Broden's grin took on a stony edge. "Och, only the lasses who have blood runnin' in their veins rather than ice water."

Quinn chuckled and winked at Skye, who flushed a becoming pink.

Kendra narrowed her eyes until only the irises were visible. "Ye great sod—"

"Kendra Eislyn Olive MacKay!" Mother's stern exclamation finally cowed her. "That will be enough. I'll remind you, we have a guest, and such vulgar speech is never acceptable from a lady."

Liam made a mental note to find out just what had transpired between his friend and sister. And to watch Quinn like a hawk around his pretty, young cousin. Quinn was a notorious philanderer.

Like moths drawn to a flame, women fawned over him. He had his pick of the lot and seldom refrained from carnal pursuits.

Azure blue eyes shining, Skye stepped forward. "Emeline. I believe we're of nearly the same size as well. Why don't you, Kendra, and I go upstairs, and we'll see what we can do about supplying you with a temporary wardrobe?"

His mother rang for the butler. Scarcely three breaths later, Simmons entered the salon. "Ye require somethin', my lady?"

"Aye, Simmons. We have the pleasure of another guest. Please prepare the—" Her gaze skittered between Liam and Emeline again. "The bedchamber beside Kendra's. Miss LeClaire can share the services of Kendra's lady's maid. Also, have baths drawn for her and Liam."

So, his mother had already perceived the attraction simmering between Liam and Emeline, and by giving her the room next to Kendra, she hoped to curtail anything untoward. She would've been wiser to put Emeline in the other wing. For Kendra's room was only four doors down and across the corridor from Liam's.

Looping her hand through Emeline's elbow, Kendra drew

her toward the door. "Come, Emeline. Ye must be exhausted after yer ordeal."

Emeline sliced Liam a speaking glance, and he gave a slight nod. They'd agreed not to discuss the matter with others and stick to the plan they'd devised. Except Broden had already broached the subject that could lead them down a very rocky path.

Liam trusted his family and friends, and his servants didn't gossip. Not if they wished to retain their positions. If anyone came calling, Emeline would stay in her chamber.

She couldn't remain secluded for long, however. They both agreed on that point. But returning to Edinburgh wasn't wise or practical. Someone had gone to tremendous effort to have her killed. For the present, it was far safer and wiser for her would-be murderer to believe she was dead.

Mayhap, he'd go to Edinburgh in her stead, but he wasn't comfortable leaving her behind either. Neither did he believe she'd sit docilely at Eytone waiting for his return. Docile wasn't a word to describe her.

"Emeline, I'll have a tray brought up for ye," his mother graciously offered. "We've already dined, but I'm sure ye're hungry."

Thank God, his mother was a kindhearted woman, for there were many who wouldn't have accepted Emeline so readily and would've cast aspersions about her being alone with Liam.

"Ye're too kind, my lady. Thank ye." Emeline allowed Kendra and Skye to tow her from the room, but, at the doorway, she cast a final undiscernible glance over her shoulder.

As asinine as it was, Liam missed her the moment she departed.

He cursed inwardly, a string of oaths that would've singed Broden's and Quinn's ears.

How had she finagled her way through the fortifications he'd so carefully erected? He'd trodden in perilous territory, and one false step would have him sinking under her spell completely.

Damn his eyes, that he could not allow.

Not and have a speck of self-respect left. Prudence demanded that while she was at Eytone Hall, he avoid her as much as feasible.

"Ye look like ye could use a dram, my friend." Broden thrust a glass with three fingers' worth of whisky toward him.

"Ye've nae idea." Shaking his head, he accepted the strong spirit.

Quinn, one elbow resting on the fireplace mantel, glanced up, a crease between his light brown brows. His gaze slid to the door and back Liam. "So what's the real story, Liam?"

Too damned perceptive as always.

His mother settled on the divan and accepted a glass of sherry from Broden. "Aye, Son. As Broden mentioned, the flash flood occurred days ago. Where have ye and that lovely young girl been in the meanwhile?"

NINE

Eight days later, Emeline strolled arm in arm with Kendra and Skye through the elaborate gardens dividing Eytone Hall's rolling lawns. Never in her life had she been so coddled. The food was excellent. The bedchamber with its molded plaster paneling and blue and white theme was like something out of a fairytale, and the borrowed clothing—though not quite an exact fit—was far superior to anything she'd ever owned.

She, Kendra, and Skye were fast becoming good friends too.

However, accustomed to being busy from the moment she awoke until she tumbled into bed, the idleness nearly drove her crazy. That and the speculative glances Lady Penderhaven, Broden, and Quinn sent her way regularly. She was dying to know just what Liam had told them.

Why were his friends still here, anyway?

It certainly wasn't her place to pose the question, but they seemed perfectly at home. Neither had mentioned their intent to leave any time soon.

Except for mealtimes, and occasionally seeing him in the

distance at one task or another, she'd seen little of Liam since her arrival. He had taken her aside that first morning and informed her he'd sent his man of business to make discreet inquiries on her behalf. But other than that one instance, he'd kept his distance.

It hurt, though she scolded herself for permitting such a silly, feminine response. She assumed Liam's duties as a feudal baron kept him occupied, but the truth was that she desired to speak to him. To spend time with him. How could she miss the company of a man she'd known but a fortnight and feel neglected by his lack of attention?

If he'd wanted to convince his family there was nothing between them, his avoidance of her and cool politesse when they did encounter each other, hadn't been as successful as he'd hoped. Liam didn't appear to have noticed, however.

Her need to return to Edinburgh weighed heavily upon her as well. Furthermore, how to explain the gap in time between when the floods occurred and when they'd arrived at Eytone Hall plagued her. Thanks be to the divine powers, not another word had been mentioned about the matter.

Very peculiar, that.

For all of their obvious curiosity, Liam's family and friends had become remarkably uninterested in that succulent tidbit.

She could only assume he'd provided a satisfactory explanation. One he'd yet to share with her, and she feared she'd blunder and undo whatever it was he'd done to appease the others' inquisitiveness.

It really was most inconsiderate of him to not elucidate to her and to ignore her like a ratty cat he'd dragged home.

Why, even Prince—truly the homeliest but sweetest dog she'd ever laid eyes upon—received more attention than she did. The bedraggled beast was constantly at his side, and several times she'd caught him passing Prince a tasty morsel or stopping to pet his shaggy, mottled head.

Sighing, she bit the inside of her cheek in self-reproach and pretended to pick a speck of lint off the light green silk gown she wore.

"Och, I'm sure it grieves ye greatly to think about yer aunt." Kendra cast her a sidelong, sympathetic glance. "Liam mentioned that ye intend to return to Edinburgh to set her affairs in order."

"Aye, but I'm no' sure when that will happen." He'd warned Emeline he couldn't leave straightaway, but worry and edginess bared their tiny sharp claws and regularly dug them into her shoulders and spine, shredding her patience.

Skye, her eyes as clear and bright blue as the September sky above, smiled gently. "I cannot imagine how lost you must feel, Emeline. I've only been away from my parents for a mite over a week. I think of them constantly and miss them dreadfully." She exchanged a serious glance with Kendra. "I'm an only child, and Liam is my guardian if something should happen to them."

"Nothin' is goin' to happen to Aunt Martha or Uncle Charles, Skye." Kendra's no-nonsense tone brooked no argument. "Yer father will make a full recovery. He's too stubborn to do otherwise. Just ye wait and see."

"I pray so, and I'm so thankful I have you, Kendra, and Aunt Louisa and Liam." Skye's bravado faltered and tears swam in her eyes. She produced a brave, if somewhat tremulous, smile. "Was your aunt your only remaining relation?"

"I have distant relatives in France, but I've never met them," Emeline said. "Honestly, I have nae desire to."

"What will ye do?" Kendra's dove-gray eyes shone with concern. Who'd have thought this spirited woman would be so considerate and generous to a stranger?

"I think…" Emeline stared across the tidy, manicured gardens, contemplating the decision she'd arrived at early this morning. Musings of a certain brawny Highlander kept her thoughts tumbling pell-mell around in her head and also had kept sleep at bay. "I think I shall sell my aunt's modiste shop." She hitched a shoulder. "I have neither the skill nor the desire to operate such an establishment."

She'd sell *if* she were the beneficiary of her aunt's will. If not…

"Emeline?"

Arms linked, the three women turned as one as Liam skirted a rose-smothered arbor.

He strode across the terrace, approaching with sinuous grace that made her insides tumble and her knees unhinge. Why must he have this effect on her? His hopelessly long legs covered the distance between them in short order, and he bowed his head in greeting. "Emeline, may I have a few moments of yer time, please?"

Emeline's heart leaped with excitement and pleasure. "Of course. Please excuse me, Kendra, Skye."

The cousins linked arms and continued on their way, their heads bent near.

Liam reached Emeline, and she offered a tentative smile. "Have ye learned somethin'?"

"I prefer we spoke in the privacy of my study." Taking her elbow, he glanced over her head, and she turned to look in the direction he peered.

Kendra and Skye had given up any pretense of subtlety and stared boldly at them, their expressions speculative.

"Och, dear. Do ye suppose…?" Heat suffused her that she couldn't blame on the mild day. She jutted her chin in his sister's direction. "Ye dinna suppose they think there's somethin' between us?"

"I havena a clue what occurs in the heads of young women. Particularly that of my sister and cousin. Neither do I want to ken. The notion fairly terrifies me." He steered her toward the house, his manner brusque and businesslike once more.

Where had the caring, concerned man in the cottage gone? This man was a stranger.

"Thank God, ye're a woman with a sensible head upon her shoulders," he muttered.

Aye, sensible. Practical. Ordinary.

A few minutes later and unexpectedly nervous, she sat in a comfortable green and gold brocade armchair in front of his impressive mahogany desk. She hadn't been in the study before, and the chamber bore Liam's presence like a mantle.

Attired in a tobacco-brown jacket, a plaid waistcoat, and breeches—rather than trews or a kilt—he presented a striking feature. His hair and beard had been trimmed, creating a rather dashing, swashbuckler's mien. The man fairly left her breathless with a single glance, and she distracted herself by examining his male dominion.

Dark wood paneling covered the walls and matching shelves paralleled the green marble fireplace. Ancient Scottish weaponry, targes, and two full suits of armor adorned the masculine room. No fire crackled in the hearth, but thick gold cords tied back the deep forest green draperies festooning the two tall windows. Sunlight spilled into the austere chamber, adding a degree of welcome and warmth he hadn't offered.

"I wanted ye to see this straightaway." He pushed a newssheet across the desk and pointed to an article.

The headline read: *POPULAR FRENCH MODISTE FLASH FLOOD VICTIM*

Emeline inhaled sharply and clasped her throat. She pulled the sheet closer, swiftly reading the first paragraph. "Och, they found Aunt Jeneva's body." Brows drawn together, she glanced up. "How did they ken who she was?"

"I dinna ken."

Something in his voice raised an alarm, and trepidation skittered down her spine.

"Read the rest, lass," he encouraged.

Heiress Emeline LeClaire is still missing and feared dead.

"There's been a mistake." She sagged back into the chair and pointed at the newspaper. "I'm no' an heiress. I'm illegitimate."

Liam skirted his desk and sank into the chair beside her. He took her icy hand between his warm palms, and she wanted to crawl into his lap and beg him to help her make sense of this.

"Em, what if ye're an heiress? Perhaps yer aunt didna ken. Perhaps she did. But if ye are, that would explain why someone targeted ye. And this..." he said, tapping the paper with his fingertip, "might well be a ruse to flush ye out."

She gulped, fear burrowing into her stomach. Would a killer go to such an extreme?

He scowled, his handsome features transforming to a seasoned warrior's fierceness. "There's even a reward for news of ye. I'd say someone grows desperate or is runnin' out of time."

Time for what?

She shook her head, unable to comprehend what the newspaper claimed. Mouth pursed and jaw set, she lifted the newssheet and read the entire article. Three times.

"It says here that they continue to look for me. Precisely who are *they*?" She met his concerned gaze, fear pulsing through her. "Liam, I need to ken the truth. I need to ken what this is all about. To find out who these people are." She shoved the newssheet away. "Perhaps..." She glanced out the window panes to the terrace dotted with pots filled with greenery, feeling more alone than she ever had in her entire isolated life. "I'll even need to travel to France."

The notion terrified rather than excited her.

"I dinna want to mention it in front of Skye, but France isna a safe place to visit right now. There's plague there," he informed her gently.

God above. Plague? Poor Skye. If her father...

"Perchance, ye had kin that succumbed, and that's why ye inherited," he offered.

Could that be true?

Aunt Jeneva had been utterly ashamed of Emeline's bastardry. But she had mentioned that distant cousin and hinted Emeline should consider marrying him. It had struck her as odd then, and even more so now.

Surely that meant her aunt had corresponded with family recently.

Mayhap she could hire a companion to accompany her on the journey.

How could she without sufficient funds?

The paltry amount in Aunt Jeneva's purse wouldn't begin to cover the expense. But her aunt had money hidden in Edinburgh. Straightening her spine and lifting her chin, she made a decision.

"Liam, I'm returnin' to Edinburgh. The answers are there. I'm certain of it." She tapped her chin with her forefinger. "My aunt hid money in her shop, and any important documents will be there as well. However, I believe it prudent to travel under an assumed name. I shall be Margaret Wilson."

He scratched his forehead, then ran his hands over his beard. His gorgeous gray eyes narrowing to shrewd slits, he gave a thoughtful nod. "I think ye're right. We can leave in two days."

"Ye mean it?" Relief flooded her and grateful tears stung her eyes. "Ye'll go with me?"

She hadn't dared hope, and pride prevented her from asking. He'd done so much already. Truthfully, she didn't want to leave him and dreaded returning to Edinburgh and all the memories awaiting her there. Nevertheless, she must get to the bottom of whatever was going on. It was impossible to go on with her life until she did.

"*Jo*, I told ye I wouldna abandon ye."

A tear dribbled from the corner of her eye.

"Dinna cry." His voice grew rough, and he brushed her cheek with his finger. "I canna bear to see ye distressed."

A frisson spiraled outward from his touch and another coiled low in Emeline's belly. She fought the urge to close her eyes and rub her face against his hand.

Why did he have this power over her?

Why must her heart yearn for a broken, wounded man incapable of loving anymore?

No, not incapable—unwilling. Liam's wife had ruined him. Such ire heated her blood at the injustice that Emeline bit down hard on her lip.

He cleared his throat and dropped his hand to his knee. His expression became meditative again. "I'll open up the house in Edinburgh. I think we should ask Kendra, Skye, Quinn, and Broden, as well as Mother to come along. She can act as a chaperone, and she'll want to oversee the servants, in any event. It will be safer for ye there, and nae one will notice one more person if we arrive *en masse*. Ye can travel as one of the housemaids."

Such a production would be sure to draw attention, wouldn't it? Although, he had a valid point about her blending into the chaos. Or mayhap, he wanted all of those people around because he wanted to make sure they were never alone together.

That hurt. Far more than she could admit to herself.

Rife with reluctance, she bit her lower lip. "I'm loath to ask yer family and friends to inconvenience themselves in such a manner." She was also horribly conflicted about him. As much as she wanted to spend time in his company—wanted so very much more—his presence was sweet torture.

In this vast house and even vaster rolling lawns and zealously attended gardens, she might admire him from afar. However, in a smaller house, keeping her powerful feelings masked would prove substantially more problematic.

At the moment, the modest, uncomplicated life of a humble seamstress held great appeal.

Liam released a sound, half-snort and half-laugh, drawing her from her reveries. As always, her heart kicked up a notch when he laughed. He should do so more often.

She'd love to be the one who caused his happiness and make him enjoy life again. But how did one win the heart of a man determined to rebuff love? A man so wounded that he rejected and scoffed at the very principle of love?

"Kendra will be thrilled," he said. "And I think Skye could use the distraction. Her father is gravely ill. Mother, on the other hand, hasna been to Edinburgh in years, so she may initially be a mite reluctant."

"But yer friends? They dinna ken me. Why would they help?" Emeline asked.

"Quinn lives for intrigue, and he has connections that can be verra valuable for things like this. Broden is like a brother to me, and I trust him with my life. He kens I'd do the same for him if he asked. They've stayed on here at my behest to help guard ye."

Well, that answered that question.

"If ye've nae objection, I'd like to send word to Graeme and Camden Kennedy as well as Logan Rutherford and Coburn Wallace apprisin' them of what's occurred. I believe they could be of tremendous help as well."

So many? Was that really necessary?

She searched his beloved face, reading the concern and determination there. She must trust him in this. If only he would trust her with his heart. "I've been meanin' to write Berget and Arieen as well. I just wasna sure what exactly I should say since we dinna want them to ken about my aunt's murder."

He rubbed his nose, looking slightly abashed. "I already

told my mother, Quinn, and Broden the truth about the murder and our stay at the cottage. I felt they should ken, given we might need to protect ye. I didna think Kendra and Skye needed to ken. It would only upset them. Mother told me she made it clear they are no' to discuss the flash flood with ye."

A sparrow swooped in to perch on a stone bench situated against a dry rock wall outside the study. Nervous and curious, it peered through the window panes, cocking its tiny head.

Emeline envied the small creature its freedom and lack of worries.

"I'll ask the others to meet us here the day after tomorrow. In the meanwhile, we need to formulate a plan." He flicked the edge of the folded paper. "I believe this is significant. Emeline, and I suspect ye may verra well have a relative who dinna want ye to inherit."

"I canna believe it. Why wouldna my aunt have said somethin'? Surely she must've kent." Tears blurred her vision and familiar grief crushed her chest.

It was an awful thing to be alone in the world, not knowing who to trust and not having anyone upon who she could rely. Except for this man who, out of the goodness of this nature, had stepped in to help her. And now, on her behalf, he'd impose upon his family and friends as well.

She searched his impenetrable eyes, seeking any hint of the passionate man who'd held her in his arms and kissed her so ravenously in the cottage. The man she would have willingly given herself to had she not been certain remorse and regret would've assailed him afterward.

Once more, Liam had barricaded himself behind those walls of indifference, and though he was kind and well-meaning, she hadn't caught a glimpse of that tender man again.

Deep in the most secret places of her heart, the tiniest spark glowed that, perhaps, she meant something to him. Because he'd been hurt and scared, he mightn't recognize it himself, but what if she could fan the ember into flame?

What if she were daring enough to woo this Highland warrior and help him heal? To put the past behind him and look to the future? To learn to trust and love again?

Did she have the gumption? Could she take the chance, even if she failed?

Emeline inhaled on a silent sob. Scalding tears tracked down her cheeks for what he'd suffered, the loss of her aunt, and the base fear for her life that hadn't subsided, leaving her tense and vulnerable.

He caressed her cheek with his thumbs and pressed a kiss to her temple. "Dinna cry, *jo*. I canna bear to see ye so wretched."

"I regret inconveniencin' ye again, Liam." She quirked her mouth into a sad, wry smile. "I have nothin' to offer in return."

He lifted her hand and, after turning it over, kissed her wrist. A thrill jolted to her elbow and skated up to her shoulder. How she craved his touch.

Bending near, he skimmed his firm mouth across hers. He tasted of whisky and raspberries. "I dinna expect anythin' in return. Let me do this for ye."

"Why?" She detected a glimpse of warmth in his quicksilver eyes that he tried so hard to hide.

"Because I quite like rescuin' ye." He gave her a boyish grin and dropped a kiss onto her nose.

The smile bending her mouth held hope. "And I quite like bein' rescued by ye."

She'd like much more too. *Much more.* But she needed to proceed cautiously, else chance losing Liam forever.

His attention gravitated to her mouth, and he leaned close once more. The heat of his body beckoned a powerful, irresistible summons.

Trembling with need, she closed her eyes, tilting her chin up in silent invitation. Just as he settled his wonderful mouth upon hers and she twined her arms around his neck, spreading her fingers through his pitch-black hair, a single sharp rap echoed at the door.

As if branded by a fire-heated sword, Liam jerked upright. His breathing rasped harsh and loud as he stood and swiftly went around to the other side of the desk.

Disoriented, Emeline struggled to bring her arousal under control and don an appearance of equanimity.

"Emeline?" He observed her, waiting for her to compose herself.

Head tilted, she schooled her features into blandness. "I'm fine. Answer the knock."

His mouth pressed into a thin line, he called, "Aye?"

The door opened and Simmons stepped inside. "Sir, Graeme Kennedy is here to see ye. He says, 'tis most urgent. Otherwise, I wouldna have interrupted ye."

His gaze slid to Emeline, and, to her credit, she managed to return his curious regard with a benign expression. At least, she prayed to all the saints that she looked unaffected and he wouldn't notice her high color.

"He says it pertains to Miss LeClaire."

TEN

Edinburgh
Five days later

Pulling the shade aside an inch, Liam leaned forward and examined the bustling shopping district from the carriage window. The tasteful businesses lining the crowded, cobbled wynd invited wealthy patrons to step within and explore.

He fixed his attention on a cobalt blue door belonging to a building on the corner. The white numbers twenty-four stood out in bold relief against the bright background of Jeneva LeClaire's modest establishment. An elegant dark blue oval sign hanging from a slightly rusty black scrolled bracket read, *La Chic Modiste,* as it swung gently in the breeze.

Nothing suspicious met his initial surveillance, but, as a seasoned fighter, he knew how deceiving appearances could be. Two women dressed in the height of fashion entered Harper & Morris Haberdashery directly to the left of *La Chic Modiste.*

Logan Rutherford and Coburn Wallace had already questioned Mrs. Morris. She admitted readily to speaking to a Frenchman and telling him the LeClaires had journeyed to the Highlands. In fact, she'd been most forthcoming, offering succulent tidbits about nearly every merchant on the street.

Beside him, Emeline sat rigidly straight and so tense he worried she'd shatter with each dip of the carriage wheels. The rich green of her borrowed cloak accented her pearly skin and the bronze hues of her luxurious hair. The fabric also made the gold flecks in her eyes sparkle, despite her solemnness.

As always, her exquisiteness bemused him. He'd known his fair share of beautiful women—including his wife—but they'd all been forgettable.

Emeline alone had imprinted her essence on his very soul.

Like him, she preferred to wear her hair unfashionably natural, free of wigs and powders. And in her case, she foreswore the lace caps most women topped their hair with as well. It was just another trivial way they were companionable. Another to add to an ever-growing list, convincing him more each day how well-suited they were.

It had been an excruciatingly long time since he'd harbored such optimism. But in the days they'd shared in the cottage, and the time she'd been at Eytone Hall, he'd come to realize she'd brought meaning back to his life.

He had reason to get up every morning.

They'd arrived in Edinburgh late in the afternoon two drizzly days ago. He hadn't formally opened the house since Kristin's death, and the sight of seven Highlanders on horseback, four coaches, and three loaded wagons heralding the grand arrival of Baron Penderhaven's household had met with frequent curious stares and brazen gawking.

Attired as a maid, and having moved to one of the

servants' equipages at their last stop, Emeline—her head covered by a coarse woolen gray cloak's hood—had been bustled into the house amid the other staff straightaway.

She'd held Prince's lead to give credence to her disguise as well as provide protection. The lumbering dog was huge, and even though he was gentle as a newborn lamb, his sheer size and scruffy appearance intimidated all but those who knew him.

Liam's mother, Kendra, Skye, as well as his male friends, had made a praiseworthy pretense of disembarking their coaches and mounts. Making themselves as conspicuous as possible, they'd chatted, stretched their legs, and fussed over their possessions, drawing all the attention and permitting the servants to disappear into the house unobtrusively.

Since meeting Emeline, the unpleasant memories and private wounds from his life with Kristin had increasingly faded, until days went by without her invading his thoughts. Not so his wee children, but the pain wasn't quite as debilitating as it had been even mere weeks ago.

For the first time in five years, he dared consider a different future from the one he'd adopted after his bairns' deaths. A future with a gentle and incomparable woman.

A woman who made his soul sing and who gave his life meaning again.

Out of habit, he brushed his hand over his face, forgetting for a second he'd shaved his beard and also shorn his mane a few inches. His hair still hung well past his coat collar.

Emeline had expressed how much she liked his hair, and since he wasn't going to start wearing wigs anytime soon, he'd left the majority of the length to please her.

The expression of delighted surprise, and then the intense

longing that had flashed across Emeline's face when first she saw him clean-shaven, made his groin contract with overwhelming need.

He fully expected the elitist denizens to speculate why he'd descended on Edinburgh at this unfashionable time of year. But he and his mother had settled on the ruse that they were officially introducing Kendra to Society as a promised birthday present.

Never mind that she'd attended other functions previously. Or that balls, routs, and other assemblies were few and far between in October. Or that Kendra's first and twentieth birthday wasn't until next month.

No one would dare speculate in his presence what the MacKays were up to. Although he'd bet Deri much chin-wagging would commence behind their backs. Gossip was the lifeblood of High Society.

Thankfully, right before they'd departed, word had come that Skye's father was slowly recovering. Aunt Martha deemed it best that Skye remained with her aunt and cousins for the foreseeable future as two servants had now fallen ill.

Emeline swallowed audibly and made a small sound of distress, wrenching Liam back to the present. Her fingers crept into his hand, and she clutched it as if it were a lifeline tossed to her in raging seas. The trust she put in him lanced his heart, but rather than leaving it wounded and oozing blood, it strengthened his resolve to make her his.

God, how he esteemed her audacity, her boldness, and her bravery every bit as much as he venerated her kindness and gentleness. He loved the way her eyes lit up when she was excited, the way her dark lashes fanned her satiny cheek, the blush of her lips, her melodious laugh, and her utterly delightful giggle.

There was nothing he didn't adore about Emeline LeClaire, and he hoped to tell her that soon. Mayhap, even tonight. Was it too soon to ask her to be his wife?

He thought of the ring box tucked in his bedside table drawer. Not a family heirloom, but a ring selected because it reminded him of her. The twelve white diamonds surrounded a chocolate-brown diamond, almost the same shade as her brilliant rich-brandy eyes.

Predictably, she'd insisted on accompanying him today. It was her right, and he'd conceded without an argument.

"I'm still on pins and needles," she said, her voice not quite steady as she gripped his hand. "I have been ever since Laird Kennedy arrived at Eytone Hall and said those men had been at Killeaggian Tower prying around about Aunt Jeneva and me. No doubt, Mrs. Morris eagerly filled their ears about our whereabouts."

She had no idea the fountain of information Mrs. Morris had proven to be.

Emeline's winged brows dipped together as she pulled her pink mouth into a thin ribbon.

"She's such a busybody and a gossip, but she was also Aunt Jeneva's friend. As our closest neighbor, it only seemed reasonable that Aunt asked her to watch the shop and feed Felix while we were away." Her graceful mouth curved the merest bit upward in a winsome manner. "Honestly, the cat spends as much time at Mrs. Morris' as he did with Aunt Jeneva. I imagine I'll just let her keep him now. Especially since I haven't yet decided what I'll do."

A wistful note leeched into her voice. Through no fault or

action of hers, her life had been turned upside down. He could sympathize in that respect. Look how long it had taken him to put his life to rights.

He'd expected Emeline wouldn't be satisfied sitting docilely in the tidy but narrow four-story house with his mother and sister, embroidering or reading while he searched her aunt's apartments and shop. And that was why the Kennedy brothers rode an inconspicuous distance behind the coach while Rutherford, Wallace, McGregor, and Catherwood were to have come separately.

They should already be in position, awaiting his and her arrival as planned.

Wallace and Catherwood watched the rear of the building, Rutherford and McGregor the front, and the Kennedys would accompany Emeline and Liam inside. Each Highlander was an experienced warrior, but a shroud of unease lay dense and weighty over him nevertheless.

The carriage rocked to a stop and then bounced as one of the coachmen descended.

"Lass, the key?" Liam gave her fingers a reassuring squeeze and he held out the palm of his other hand.

Wordlessly, Emeline passed him the heavy brass key.

"Ye must promise to do exactly as I say, Em," he said gently but firmly. "No arguin' or hesitatin'. Yer life may depend upon it."

Her eyes absent their usual brightness, she cast a covert glance to the shade-covered window and nodded. "I ken. I shall."

Bloody hell. How her damn trepidation infuriated him. Not that he directed the ire toward her, but to the miscreant that had dared threaten her. The poltroon who'd hired others to do his dirty work and was such a coward that he targeted defenseless women.

"I'm goin' to descend first," he said, reining in his ire. He must keep his wits honed and not permit any distractions, even in thought. "I want to make sure Logan and Broden are stationed outside before ye alight. I've nae doubt that the establishment is bein' watched. Even now, 'tis possible our arrival has been marked."

Emeline nervously licked her lower lip, her stunning umber-colored eyes wide and apprehensive.

"Please do be careful, Liam," she urged, her voice low and husky with her concern. "We ken what these people are capable of. I dinna want ye or the others hurt."

Cupping her shoulders, he pressed a long, fervent kiss to her forehead, saying with his actions what he wasn't quite ready to say with words.

That he'd die before he'd allow any harm to come to her.

That he still wrestled with demons from his past, but he believed, with her by his side, he might be able to face the future again.

That she'd set up home in his heart and had commandeered his spirit, and his life was no longer his but hers to do with what she willed.

She was his life. His breath. His everything.

He'd tell her those things soon. *Verra soon.*

Even as a callow youth who'd lusted after the English beauty that had become his first wife, he hadn't experienced this all-consuming need. To make Emeline his. To take her to his bed and love and worship her until they forgot all else but each other.

He'd need to tell her about the foolishness that had

resulted in his forced marriage though. His conscience wouldn't allow him to court her otherwise.

"Liam?"

He started, realizing he hadn't eased her worry.

"I can defend myself, *mo chroí. M'anam. Mo grá.*" *My heart. My soul. My love.* He patted the dirk at his waist, rather than in his boot, and then his sword. The others had guns as well. "Dinna fash yerself, *leannan.*"

Her turbulent umber eyes rounded impossibly wider, vulnerability and an unspoken question in their depths at the endearment. "I canna help but fret."

She *was* his sweetheart. *Aye, and more.* Much more, despite his determination otherwise. He started to turn away, but she clasped his forearm. "Liam?"

He turned back, eyebrows taut.

To his utter astonishment and delight, she scooted across the seat and pressed a soft kiss to his scarred cheek. The puckered flesh throbbed where her sweet mouth had touched the bunched flesh. She laid a hand on his other clean-shaven cheek.

"I couldna bear it if somethin' happened to ye. Nothin' in there"—Emeline gestured toward the quaint shop entrance—"is worth ye riskin' yer life for. *Nothin'.*" Her grip on his forearm tightened.

His heart was so full that he wanted to shout his jubilation from Eytone Hall's gables. Instead, he slid an arm around her slender shoulders, drawing her near, and kissed her deeply and thoroughly. She collapsed into him, returning the kiss with inexperienced enthusiasm.

The blood rushing in his ears, he harnessed his passion. Caution and common sense demanded they stop. When he finally raised his head, he gritted his teeth against the lust surging through his loins.

Emeline's eyelids fluttered open, and she gifted him with a radiant smile. The luster of her sweetly curved lips toppled his resolve. As always, her loveliness clobbered him with the force of a bludgeon, but it was the unguarded affection shimmering in her innocent gaze that shook his foundation.

Now wasn't the time to contemplate the revelation, however. Retrieving the documents and whatever else she deemed necessary, as well as keeping her safe, were his primary concerns. He would consider this unexpected but highly prized discovery later. When he'd completed this self-appointed mission.

Unbeknownst to her, he and his six friends had set a trap for her assailants. If all went as anticipated, she'd be free from the fear that had dogged her since that fateful afternoon she'd almost been murdered.

He recalled, again, how brave and majestic she'd been facing down her attackers that day. A seasoned battlefield warrior couldn't have been more courageous.

Whoever the scoundrel was hunting her, he had resources and money. Besides the drivers Liam had killed, there had also been the two men who'd been snooping around Killeaggian Tower. God only knew how many others were in his employ and, undoubtedly, watching *Le Chic Modiste* even now.

The carriage door swung open and, canting his head to the driver—also armed—Liam descended. He deliberately stood in the opening, blocking any curious passersby or would-be assassins' view of the interior. With indolent casualness, he yawned and, through hooded eyes, scrutinized the area.

"Stay alert," he advised the coachmen. "And be in your seat, ready to leave the instant we emerge from the shop."

"Aye, sir," the driver said, his sharp-eyed gaze scanning the area.

Liam wrinkled his nose. Edinburgh stank.

Overpopulated and crowded, the city was a cesspool of excrement, rodents, and refuse. Nonetheless, pedestrians strolled along, occasionally picking their way around or stepping neatly over rubbish or horse manure.

Equestrians clattered past atop their mounts. A variety of conveyances rumbled up and down the busy street, and grubby, thin-faced urchins darted here and there.

Making a show of examining the sullen clouds for signs of rain, he tilted his head upward. He took note of the rooftops, some stacked six stories high in the distance. Whoever spied upon Jeneva LeClaire's shop did so discreetly. At least thus far.

Armed in much the same manner as he, except they also bore firearms, Graeme and Camden Kennedy sauntered forward. Every one of the Highlanders he'd asked to assist him had done so without hesitation.

After exchanging a casual greeting for the benefit of anyone spying upon them, the threesome formed a semi-circle before the open coach door.

The coachman assumed a position halfway between the shop and the conveyance while the other driver, atop his seat, swept his keen gaze back and forth, focused and alert.

"Come, Emeline." Liam reached his hand inside the equipage, and she placed her palm in his, permitting him to assist her to the ground. The trio immediately closed ranks around her, making it impossible for anyone to approach. The men boasted large frames. While Emeline wasn't petite, they dwarfed her as they moved as one to the entrance.

"Berget sends her greetin', Miss LeClaire," Graeme said with a kind quirk of his mouth. "She hopes ye'll pay a visit soon."

Leave it to him to try to put Emeline at ease.

Face pinched and appearing as if she might cast up her breakfast, she fashioned a small smile in response.

Liam's brows crashed together as he inserted the key into the brass lock. The catch had been forced. He cast Graeme a sidelong look, saying out the side of his mouth, "The lock is broken. Someone's been here before us."

ELEVEN

The revelation came as no surprise. "The back entrance is more inconspicuous. 'Tis odd they'd choose the one facin' the main street," Liam remarked.

"There's a stout board obstructin' the back doorway, rather than a keyed entrance," Emeline said. "I imagine that's why. It would have been much too noisy to break the door down. Mrs. Morris hears *everythin'*." The last she murmured in a tone that clearly conveyed she didn't mean it as a compliment.

At once, Graeme and Camden slid their hands to their waists and grasped their dirks. Liam lifted his cocked hat and smoothed his hand over his head, a sign to the others that the establishment had been broken into and to be on guard.

Rutherford signaled to Broden, who strolled to the other side of the street and doffed his hat. A warning to Wallace and Catherwood to be vigilant.

One hand at the base of Emeline's spine, Liam ushered her in behind Graeme.

She gasped in dismay upon entering the dim interior.

"Nae! Look what they've done, the rotters!" she cried softly. Fingers to her mouth and pale but steady on her feet, she gingerly ventured forward, slowly turning her head back and forth as she took in the mayhem. "I dinna understand. What could they possibly be after? They even sliced the cushions open."

It was true.

The cushion stuffing had been ripped out and scattered pell-mell. The place was an absolute shamble. Fabric lay strewn upon the floor. Every shelf had been swept clean of its contents, and every bureau drawer emptied. The intruders had yanked the artwork from the walls, dumped out a potted fern, and tipped over the coal basket during their thorough search.

"I'll check above," Camden said before disappearing up the narrow flight of stairs situated at the back of the shop.

Emeline cast a furtive glance to the window. Tasteful midnight-blue draperies obscured the display window as well as blocked the view of any curious patrons or passersby. She pointed to an unremarkable, long cutting table against the far wall.

Speaking in a low tone, she said, "There's a board beneath a table leg that is loose. Aunt Jeneva hid anythin' of import in the space beneath it."

Graeme stepped to the door and, arms crossed, rested his back against the entrance, preventing anyone from coming inside. A handful of breaths later, Camden lumbered down the steps, a deep line between his eyebrows. "Whoever they were, they ransacked the upstairs livin' quarters and bedchambers as well."

"I expected as much," Liam said, once more grateful his friends had agreed to assist him.

The plundered establishment confirmed his suspicions about why Emeline had been targeted. Quinn and Camden had poked around a bit themselves yesterday and discovered a French aristocrat had arrived in Edinburgh recently. Likely the very same man who'd visited the haberdashery next door.

Liam didn't believe in coincidence.

The young and *oh so, debonair* Frenchman—according to Mrs. Morris—was a minor noble named Jean Claude Gagneux. Since his arrival, he'd been making the social rounds. Although, no one could specifically recall his inquiring after or mentioning Emeline or her aunt.

Smart bastard. Liam would give him that.

Quinn had also inquired at the *The Edinburgh Evening Courant* regarding the heiress article. The reporter who'd written it had gone missing a week ago—just hadn't shown up for work one day.

Likely dead. The assassin had left no loose threads.

No one else at the paper could—*or would*—provide any information, including the sources for his story or how Jeneva's body had been found or identified. Quinn had, however, learned an unmarked grave in Greyfriars Kirkyard marked her final resting place.

Liam suspected the assassin had sent men to investigate why the killers assigned to drive the coach and kill Emeline hadn't returned. They'd come upon the coach, Jeneva's corpse, or mayhap both. Damn lucky for them if that were the case.

The *Courant's* editor might know something as well, but he was too terrified to reveal what he knew, or a bribe kept his mouth shut. Or, perhaps, he'd approved the story for sensationalism. He wouldn't be the first or the last newspaperman to look the other way to sell a few extra newssheets.

Camden took a position beside the window, covertly edging the fabric aside to peek out the glass. "Nothin' suspicious lookin' yet."

Liam made short work of pulling the table away from the wall. "Which board?" His nape hair stood on end, his warrior's instinct detecting danger. "Graeme, Camden, be at the ready. I dinna have a good feelin'."

"Aye," they answered in unison, tugging their guns free.

Her plump lower lip clamped between her teeth, Emeline studied the scraped and scuffed floorboards for a moment. Squatting, she pointed. "There. That's the one."

Hunkered down, Liam used the tip of his dirk to pry the oak plank upward. It gave way, making a soft, scritching sound.

With the draperies closed and no candlelight either, viewing the inside of the small compartment proved difficult. However, without hesitation, Emeline kneeled and reached her gloved hand within. She withdrew an octagon-shaped satinwood inlaid box. "Everythin's in here."

Giving a severe tilt of his head in acknowledgment, Liam reached for the board, intending to replace it in case the robbers returned. He didn't want them to know about the secret hideaway. That would give them more reason to find Emeline. Something shiny caught the corner of his eye, and he leaned closer.

"What's this?" Unease knotting his neck and shoulders, he extended a hand into the hole and clasped a hard object. He withdrew a rectangular metal casket-type box.

A fine line creasing her forehead, Emeline sent him an

astonished look. "I dinna ken what that is. I've never seen it before."

Liam's gut told him this was what the assassin was after. He couldn't guess why Jeneva LeClaire hadn't told her niece about the case. But placing the small chest in the place Emeline knew she kept her valuables meant she wanted to ensure Emeline found the box if something happened.

"We dinna have time to go through these now." He swiveled to Camden and flicked a hand toward the hole in the floor. "Close this up and put the table back. I'm takin' Emeline upstairs to collect anythin' she needs."

The warning bells in his head pealed raucously louder once they reached the upper story, and she glided into the nearest bedchamber. He strode down the narrow corridor to the room at the far end, past the living apartments.

"This was yer aunt's bedchamber?" he called.

Emeline poked her head out the doorway. "Aye."

He peeked inside, not surprised to see the room as ravaged as the lower level had been. He spoke over his shoulder. "Would your aunt have hidden anythin' of value in here?"

"I dinna think so." Eyes narrowed in consideration, Emeline shook her head. "Aunt Jeneva was paranoid. She wouldna even move the table below until after she'd hung an extra panel across the window, locked the doors, and waited until the wee mornin' hours."

It turned out she had good reason to be distrustful. Which, again, begged the question: what did Jeneva LeClaire know and when did she know it?

Swiftly retracing his steps, he took mental note of Emeline's progress before surreptitiously glancing out her bedchamber window.

Broden, hat lowered and ankles crossed, lounged against a milliner's shop across the street.

Liam couldn't see Logan Rutherford from this angle.

He veered Emeline a quick glance.

She swiftly shoved a few more garments into her valise. After searching the floor for a handful of breaths, she spotted her hairbrush. She seized it and plopped it atop the pile inside the valise. Her furrowed brows and pursed mouth were silent testament to her distress as she cast a wary eye about her chamber.

He returned his attention to the wynd below.

Hell.

Two scruffy men ambled down the cobblestones. Another unkept pair of scunners joined them. Each looked like a down-on-his-luck beggar rather than mercenaries. A calculated ploy so Liam would underestimate them, or were they the only riffraff the Frenchman could find to do his dirty work?

Hopefully, the latter.

The miscreants shuffled to a stop several feet away from the modiste shop. One, attired in a too-big, moth-eaten coat spat, and another who wasn't wearing stockings picked his teeth while they listened to something their apparent leader said.

Broden casually pushed his tam up his forehead, his flinty gaze trained on the quartet. He drew upright as two more unsavory reprobates ambled toward the foursome.

Christ.

"Emeline, we need to go. I'll send someone back to collect the rest of yer belongin's."

She raised her head, a question in her eyes.

"We must leave at once." He wasn't going to tell her about the men outside. She'd find out soon enough.

He took the valise from her. After placing the containers from beneath the floorboard inside, he closed the top with a quiet *snick*. He tapped the bag's handles. "I believe the contents of those boxes are the most critical. But just in case there's somethin' else here we've overlooked, I'll ask Logan and Coburn to thoroughly search both levels later. If that's acceptable to ye."

Even if it wasn't.

Sadness crimped the corners of her eyes and pulled her dainty mouth downward. "Aye. 'Tis still so hard to believe she's really gone, that I'll never see her again. And that someone—God only kens who—is so vile they'd do this and try to kill me too."

"I ken, *leannan*. I ken." He drew her into a swift hug, kissing her forehead. She leaned into him, her cheek against his chest, and he closed his eyes for two blinks, savoring the moment. "Come, *jo*. We must be off."

He turned her toward the landing, then preceded her down the stairs.

Graeme stepped forward. "Liam, I dinna like this. Somethin' feels off."

Camden nodded in agreement, his steely gaze repeatedly sweeping from the front door to the window to the back entrance.

"It is. I spied six men from the window upstairs. Broden noticed them too, so he'll have alerted the others." Liam made certain to keep the alarm from seeping into his voice. He'd never known Emeline to dissolve into histrionics but didn't want to chance her doing so now.

"Liam, why didna ye say somethin'?" The color fled her face, except for two crimson spots on her cheeks. "I told ye no' to take any chances."

Merely coming to Edinburgh had been a huge risk. Nevertheless, if there were answers to be found, he'd vow they'd be in the valise she clutched to her chest.

"We're leavin' now. Dinna worry."

"Do stop sayin' that. I can nae more stop frettin' than ye can stop eatin'," Emeline snapped, the strain testing her self-possession. "And we both ken that is never happenin'."

"Och, an impossibility, to be sure." Graeme chuckled, earning him a sour look from Liam.

"Do exactly as I say, Emeline—"

"Liam MacKay!" Her irritation had transformed into outright anger. "I am no' a bairn, nor am I a lackwit. I'd appreciate bein' asked and no' ordered about."

This fiery-tempered version of Emeline was breathtaking. Nevertheless, her tender sensibilities would have to suffer a bit of bruising.

He speared the Kennedys a glance. "As before, we'll keep Emeline between us. Graeme, ye take the bag. Camden, open the door and take a look around. They'll be to yer left." He caught each of their eyes. "Ye ken what do."

Camden complied with a severe downward thrust of his chin.

"I can carry the valise—" Emeline started to object, a mutinous tilt to her pert chin that Liam hadn't seen before.

"If ye need to lift yer skirts to run, I'd rather ye had both hands free, lass," he said, holding onto his patience by a thread.

"Oh," she murmured, taken aback, her expression contrite.

She obviously hadn't considered that possibility. God knew he had. He angled his head toward Graeme, and, wordlessly, she extended the valise.

The four of them had no sooner stepped from the shop than the half-dozen armed ruffians descended upon them, weapons drawn. Matrons screamed, mothers clutched their children close, and terrified people scattered in all directions. Reeking of unwashed bodies and stale ale, the band of hirelings approached, menace in each confident, swaggering step.

As Liam had planned in the event something of this nature occurred, Camden swept a startled Emeline into his arms and bolted toward the carriage a few feet away.

Graeme followed, hot on his heels, wielding his gun. His horse stood beside the carriage, and the coachmen were poised to take off, their pistols drawn and pointed directly at the scourge determined to kill Emeline.

"Nae. What are ye doin'? I willna leave him! Put me down," she screamed, pounding Camden's back. "Li...am! Nae. Nae! I canna leave him."

Without slowing his pace, Camden grunted, "Sorry, lass. I gave my word."

"Shite, dinna let her escape again!" one gunman shouted, aiming his firearm at Camden's back.

Liam slammed his hand down on the cur's forearm while smashing his fist into the man's face. Dropping his blunderbuss, the sod crumpled into an insensate heap.

That's one— Five more to go.

Camden all but tossed Emeline inside the carriage before diving in after her. His gun drawn, Graeme threw the bag inside the equipage and jumped atop his mount. As the carriage sprang forward, the door still gaping wide open, Liam growled his satisfaction.

Emeline was safe. For now.

The other five louts advanced on him, and he grinned as he yanked his dirk from his waist and his sword from its sheath. "Come on then, ye devil's spawn."

He'd enjoy seeking vengeance on Emeline's behalf.

"Ye're outnumbered, ye bloody cockscum," snarled a man missing his front teeth. He gave a maniacal laugh, spittle forming on the corner of his mouth. "The lass will nae get away. That fancy Frenchman will no' stop until she's dead."

"Hold yer wheesht, ye idiot," bellowed his compatriot. "Nae one's to ken about him."

"It willna make a difference," the first ruffian argued, his beady gaze glinting with wrath. "Who's this bastard goin' to tell when he's dead?" He snickered as if he'd made a clever jest.

"Ye're assumin' ye can kill me, ye whoremonger." Weapons at the ready, Liam inched backward.

Like a pack of rabid, snarling wolves, they advanced toward him.

One wearing an incongruent vibrant purple silk and gold waistcoat beneath his impossibly filthy brown jacket elbowed another in the side and gave a malevolent chuckle. "Numpty sot still disna get it. There are five of us and one of him."

"I'm surprised ye can count that high," Liam said dryly, skewing his mouth into a mocking smile.

"Actually, ye tosspots, there are five of us as well," Brogdon drawled, a wicked grin creasing his face. He enjoyed a brawl more than any man Liam knew.

Jaw slack, the thug swung around.

Logan, Quinn, and Coburn flanked Broden, each with murder etched upon their harsh features.

"I want them alive," Liam growled before lunging forward to take down the first man.

The hired thugs were no match for Liam and his friends. In short order, three more lay unconscious, and a fourth hunched upon the ground, supporting his broken arm. The fifth scumbag squirmed as Liam pressed his fingers hard into the man's throat and shoved him against the building.

"Who hired ye?"

The man sneered in defiance, and Liam tightened his grasp.

Clawing at Liam's hand, the hireling tried to kick him.

Mrs. Morris poked her bewigged head out of the haberdashery. Upon spying Liam with a man by the throat, she uttered a strangled squeak and slammed the door shut. The rasping and clicking of three locks being secured in rapid succession almost made him grin. *Almost.*

"I'll ask ye one more time before I start breakin' bones," Liam said. "Who. Hired. Ye?"

Gray-faced and making gurgling noises, the wretch stuttered, "The...wench's...brother."

Liam loosened his grip a fraction, uncertain he'd heard correctly. Emeline had said she hadn't any kin but distant cousins.

"Brother?" He scowled and shook the wretch. "Are ye certain?"

"Aye. Aye." The man gasped and choked, his bulging eyes darting back and forth. As if he realized the game was up, he babbled, "A prissy fella named Jean Claude Gagneux. He's boardin' at the Swan and Stag at the south end of town."

The cur sitting on the ground and favoring his arm snickered. His mad-eyed gaze shifted between Liam and his friends standing guard over the other miscreants. "He kens where she's stayin' too."

Christ on the blessed cross.

Swearing beneath his breath, Liam gave the thug another hard shove before releasing him. Cradling his already bruising neck, the man slumped to the ground as Liam spun toward his friends.

"Coburn, Logan, see these Satan's spawns are turned over to the authorities," he said, swiping his hair off his forehead. "Broden, ye and Quinn, come with me. We're payin' Monsieur Gagneux a visit."

TWELVE

One, two, three, four, five, six, seven, eight, nine, ten.

Emeline pivoted and paced the other direction, deliberately counting her steps again. Doing so kept her focused and also from screaming her frustration and fear. She darted a glance at the bronze mantle clock, and the air whooshed from her lungs.

Prince, lying before the hearth, raised his head from his forepaws, watching her progress with worried pecan-brown eyes. Releasing a woeful sigh, he lowered his head once more, but his dark gaze never left her.

Three hours.

Three hours since Camden Kennedy had unceremoniously scooped her up like a sack of grain and tossed her into the carriage. Three hours since she been bustled inside the house and offered tea to soothe her frayed nerves. Three interminable hours since she'd last seen her beloved's face contorted into a battle-hardened warrior's scowl.

She marched to the window and peered out onto the street again.

Och, when I see Liam MacKay, Baron Penderhaven, again, I'll give him a piece of my mind for havin' me carted off like a hog to market.

For not telling her his insane plan to which she would have strenuously objected. For staying behind to make certain she was safely away. For putting her life before his.

Her heart contracted painfully. *Oh, Liam, ye darin', wonderful numpty.* Blinking away tears, she muttered beneath her breath, "I'll strangle him with my bare hands."

Or hug and kiss him until every last morsel of worry had dissipated.

"I'd rather like to watch that," Kendra quipped, though her flippant reply didn't hide the apprehension etched upon her fine features. She might pretend to be unaffected, but she was as worried about Liam and the others' continued absence as everyone else was.

"Kendra," her mother chided with no real censure. "Ladies dinna revel in the notion of their brothers bein' strangled. Even if they deserve it," Lady Penderhaven muttered beneath her breath.

"But, Mama, imagine it. Emeline has such dainty hands, and Liam has a neck as thick as a bull's." She gave an unapologetic shrug. "The logistics fascinate me. I doubt 'tis even possible, he's so stiff-necked."

Skye's droll chuckle brought a bit of lightness to the too-serious atmosphere. "Ye are awful, Kendra MacKay." She fared only slightly better as her tormented serviette and low sighs every few minutes attested.

"Miss LeClaire, ye shouldna be near the window," Camden advised patiently for at least the tenth time. He gave the sofa a pointed look, which she deliberately disregarded with a frosty glare and an elevated chin.

She hadn't forgiven him or his brother for their parts in hauling her away, leaving Liam to trounce those blackguards alone.

Except, as Camden had patiently explained on the wild carriage ride home, and Graeme had done again once inside the house, Liam's four other friends were there to back him up.

She felt marginally reassured until she recalled the blackguards' malicious, twisted faces. If any of those men had ever possessed a conscience—and she had her doubts they had even as wee bairns—they'd long since sold any sense of decency to the devil. Their very souls were as black as the Earl of Hell's waistcoat.

Her stomach pitched again, and she swallowed against a wave of nausea and faintness. By God, she would not succumb to womanly histrionics and weakness. She would be courageous and display fortitude, such as Liam had shown. At least, she would try to.

Graeme Kennedy, along with a trio of footmen, were stationed about the house's entrances. A flea couldn't enter the place and hope to live longer than half a second.

Where is Liam?

Every horrible scenario possible had played out like a macabre skit on a stage in Emeline's skull, and she feared she'd go mad from worry and dread. He must be all right.

He must. He must. He must, Emeline chanted to herself.

She hadn't told him she loved him at Eytone Hall. Hadn't been bold or daring enough to risk his rejection or scorn. Or worse, his cold indifference. And now—

What if it was too late? If something happened—

"My dear girl." Lady Penderhaven patted the gold and ruby cushion beside her on the divan. "Come sit. Ye're makin' me nervous and techy as a broody hen on a nest with yer pacin' and frettin'."

Naturally, Liam's mother was every bit as concerned for her son, yet she sat regal and composed. The epitome of unruffled refinement, while Emeline's lower lip had been tortured unmercifully, and the cuffs of her borrowed rose and gold gown were much worse the wear from her repeated plucking at the edges.

"Forgive me, yer ladyship." At once chagrined, Emeline fashioned a contrite upward tilt of her lips.

Again, his mother tipped her mouth into an inviting smile and indicated the cushion with another firm pat. "Come. Sit. Have a spot of tea, or do ye prefer coffee?"

"Tea, please."

Emeline plopped onto the divan in an undignified fashion, straining her ears for any hint of a familiar male voice. A specific male voice.

She absently accepted the saucer of tea Lady Penderhaven offered. Her gaze fell on the satchel, still exactly where Camden had placed it when they entered the drawing room. She'd flung Kendra's cloak over the back of the closest chair.

Precisely what did the two boxes nestled within her bag contain?

She didn't want to examine the contents with an audience, but avid curiosity had scythed her from the moment Liam had discovered the second box. Perchance, examining the items would help keep her mind off of Liam's continued absence and any number of awful reasons he was taking so long to return. She set the still hot tea down and wiped her suddenly damp palms on her skirt.

"I believe I'll retire to my chamber." She rose and, after draping the cloak across her arm and seizing the bag in a much-too-firm-grip, swept to the door. At once, Prince lumbered to his oversized feet and came to her. "I should like some time alone. Please excuse me."

Compassion and understanding softened the women's faces.

"Of course, my dear," her ladyship murmured. "We understand. This has been most tryin' for ye."

Kendra and Skye exchanged a knowing look before turning sympathetic gazes upon Emeline. "Perhaps ye should have a lie-down too," Kendra suggested, her usual mischievousness subdued. "Ye're a wee bit pale."

She also had a headache. "Aye, I may."

But not until she'd thoroughly examined every single thing in both boxes.

Camden came to her side at once. "I'll accompany ye, Miss LeClaire, and stand guard outside yer door."

Of course he would.

It made her feel like a prisoner rather than protected. However, as she'd learned during the awful ride home, Camden wouldn't give an inch. If she weren't so vexed with him, she'd have admired his loyalty and commitment to Liam.

Camden Kennedy was a man of his word. An excellent man to have as an ally. Not such an excellent fellow to have as a prison guard.

Nonetheless, she pulled a face before painting on a placid expression. "Did Liam tell ye no' to let me out of yer sight or some such balderdash?"

"Some such balderdash." An unrepentant grin tipped his mouth.

Rolling her eyes, she snorted. "Men."

Five minutes later, she sat cross-legged atop the soft turquoise coverlet on her bed. The pair of boxes lay before her and Prince sprawled beside her. As much as she was dying to know their contents, trepidation also squeezed her ribs and made her feel hot and cold all at once.

Her future may very well lay inside these unassuming containers. *My past too.*

She lifted the satinwood octagon, preferring to explore the known before the mysterious and potentially distressing. Slowly, tentatively, she raised the familiar etched lid. Nestled inside lay the leather bag of coins she'd expected, along with a black velvet cloth which she knew to contain a few pieces of jewelry: a set of ruby earrings, a string of pearls, a pair of diamond and gold hair combs, and a rather masculine looking gold ring stamped with the same emblem as atop the case.

She'd seen them all before. Knew the ruby earrings had been her mother's, and the pearls her grandmother's. Aunt Jeneva had never explained the exact origins of the hair combs and ring, but when Emeline had asked about them as a child, she had crossly muttered something about them being family tokens.

Emeline set the coin bag and jewels aside, then lifted the folded papers from within the satin-lined box. Prince cracked an eye open and, after giving the two items a baleful look, resumed his slumber.

The documents included the deed to the shop, a record of Emeline's birth—chronicled at a parish outside Edinburgh by a Father Sinclair—a pile of neatly tied letters, and a third parchment. She gingerly unrolled the slightly yellowed pages and stared down at her aunt's last will and testament. A quick perusal of the document answered one question. Aunt Jeneva had bequeathed her everything.

Tucked into the last page was a short letter addressed to her from her aunt. The paper was crisp and the ink fresh. No wax seal adorned its face either. She'd written this quite recently and possibly in haste.

Gooseflesh raised on Emeline's arms, and a shiver rippled from her nape to her waist. Her breath came in short pants as realization dawned. Had Aunt Jeneva had a premonition something was going to happen?

Prince lifted his head and whined.

"'Tis all right, boy," Emeline soothed, skimming a hand over his coarse coat.

My Dearest Emeline,

If you're reading this, then I've passed on. Hopefully, our Heavenly Father found favor with me and admitted me into His holy Kingdom. I know I haven't been as warm or affectionate in my behavior as you've needed me to be. Neither sentiment came naturally to me, but I've tried my utmost to do what was right by you.

Without you, Emeline, my life would have been a spinster's meaningless, lonely existence, and although the reasons why I came to raise you were difficult, please know that I've treasured every day you've been a part of my life.

A tear dribbled down her cheek.

How often had she questioned if Aunt Jeneva held her in any regard? She'd always felt a burden to her aunt, but now she knew beyond a doubt that Aunt Jeneva had loved her in her way. Sensing her distress, Prince crawled nearer and laid his big head in her lap, gazing at her with soulful eyes.

"I'm all right," she said, more to convince herself than the docile dog.

Sniffing, she blinked to clear her vision and read on.

I wish I could end this letter on a positive note and tell you to be happy and to live your dreams, but you must be made aware that you have a younger half-brother, Jean Claude Gagneux.

Jaw slack, Emeline's heart welled with joy. A brother? She wasn't alone after all.

He is not a good man, and that is why I encouraged you to marry a distant cousin in France.

Her euphoria dissolved as swiftly as salt in cock-a-leekie soup.

I have corresponded with our distant cousin, Pierre Durpreiz, intermittently over the years and hoped he could protect you in ways I could not. He is not aware I suggested a union between you, but if you should ever need help for any reason, do not hesitate to contact him. He will aid you in any way he can. He told me as much in his last letter.

I'm sure you've also found the second box. It contains several very important documents that only recently came into my possession. Pierre sent them, believing you should know the truth of your birth. I don't know how he came to have them, but he was a good friend of your father's. I can only conclude your father wanted you to have them and asked Pierre to assist in that endeavor.

I beg you to forgive me for not telling you. I was selfish and didn't want to lose you. Live well, Emeline. You've been an exquisite gift, and I have loved you.

Aunt Jeneva

Great fat tears fell in earnest now, cascading down Emeline's cheeks, and she fumbled for her handkerchief. She pressed the small square to her mouth. Shoulders quaking, she buried her face in Prince's neck, weeping for the aunt who'd never told her she loved her until she did so in a letter after her death. Several minutes ticked past until she wrestled her grief under control. Giving a final shuddery sob, she sat up and dabbed her face with her sodden hankie.

Aunt Jeneva's letter hadn't only intensified her curiosity but magnified her dread too.

"I have a brother." A not-so-nice brother, according to her aunt.

Emeline eyed the stack of letters tied together by a faded green ribbon. She'd reached to untie the silk tie, but the metal box beckoned. Shifting her position, she gingerly lifted the lid. An ordinary-looking packet wrapped in brown leather lay inside.

Once more, Prince had spread out on the coverlet and succumbed to sleep.

She undid the string holding the rectangle tight and unfurled the leather. The scent of leather, ink, and parchment wafted upward. The first parchment named Tron Parish, where a marriage record between Madeleine LeClaire and Antoine Gagneux was recorded.

Emeline sucked in a ragged breath, nearly dropping the parchment as she reread the flourishing script.

Oh my God and all the angels.

Her parents *had* been married. She wasn't illegitimate.

She knew exactly where Christ's Kirk at the Tron was. That's where she and Aunt Jeneva attended Sunday services. Could it be true? Could the very same parish she'd been in so many times contain the record of her parents' marriage?

Why, then, hadn't her father ever acknowledged her?

She wrinkled her forehead, more confused than ever.

Was this why Aunt Jeneva had asked for her forgiveness? For keeping this monumental secret? At one time, Emeline would've been furious at Aunt Jeneva for this deception. Now, after everything that had occurred, she couldn't bring herself to be angry at her aunt.

Eyebrows pulled together, Emeline unfurled the next document. It contained the name of a solicitor in France who had a copy of Monsieur Antoine Gagneux's Last Will and Testament. According to the scribbled note, as Gagneux's only legitimate heir, she'd been named the sole beneficiary of his substantial estate.

Her lungs stalled as she absorbed the last line.

Och, now that is certainly a reason for someone—likely my brother—to want to dispose of me.

Heart pounding and her head reeling from what she'd learned, she picked up one of the two letters between her thumb and forefinger. She didn't recognize the scrawling penmanship, yet she knew with absolute certainty her father had written it.

Inhaling a bracing breath, she broke the wax seal. A seal that exactly matched the emblem on the ring and the etching on the satinwood box. Additional proof of her heritage.

While she mightn't be able to muster anger for her aunt's deception, molten anger and frustration simmered beneath the surface for the cowardly man who'd sired her.

It further raised her ire that she should care. That this man she didn't know could cause such an unwelcome and unfamiliar reaction.

Didn't this letter prove he knew of her existence?

Yet not once in over four and twenty years had he made a single effort to contact her.

Why?

Jaw clamped to still the weird chattering of her teeth, Emeline read the letter. Exhaling her breath in a whoosh, she flopped back onto her pillows in disbelief.

She'd never have guessed the truth. Never.

Her father had loved her mother. They'd secretly married in Scotland because his family didn't approve of a disgraced comte's impoverished daughter for their son. Vowing to return, he'd left Mama with Aunt Jeneva and ventured home to tell his family the joyous news.

He hadn't kept his promise.

He'd never returned—the unconscionable bounder.

Evidently, Antoine Gagneux had led a very privileged life and had wrongly assumed, as the cherished only son, his family would come around and accept Mama as his wife.

However, threatened with disinheritance and banishment, he'd committed bigamy and conceded to an arranged marriage to a duke's daughter. He'd sired two children with her: Jean Claude, two and twenty, and Jeannette eighteen.

I have a sister too.

Was she of the same caliber as their brother?

Sadness twisted Emeline's belly. Her whole life, she'd longed to know something of her father, and such overwhelming disappointment flooded her to learn he was a poltroon of the worst sort.

He'd been aware of Emeline's birth through his lifelong friend, Pierre. Weakling that he was, however, Gagneux hadn't the courage to contact her. *Dear cowardly Papa hadna the valor of a turnip or a cabbage, it seems.* Besides, indulged and selfish, he'd suspected how infuriated Jean Claude would be to discover the truth.

How could Jean Claude not be furious? He'd expected to inherit.

So, these many years, Emeline's father had kept his despicable secret.

"What a bounder," she grumbled, causing Prince's tail to thump once. "Ye like that, do ye?"

Bounder. Cur. Blackguard. Coward. She was sorely pressed to summon a single positive moniker for her sire.

Haunted by his abandonment of Mama and her, he'd vowed to make it right and changed his will when his wife had died five years ago. By providing proof he'd been married before he exchanged vows in France, he'd relegated his other children to the status of bastards.

That had to have been awful for them. Unless—

Perhaps, it wasn't public knowledge yet. Could that be why her brother targeted her?

More befuddled and bewildered than she'd ever been, she shook her head. Not only wasn't she illegitimate, but she was also an heiress. She couldn't find a great deal of compassion for a man who was so feeble in character that he deserted his wife and committed bigamy.

All because he hadn't loved Mama more than his wealth and position.

Scant doubt remained who had the most to gain if she were dead. She remembered the second letter. Without rising, she stretched to clasp the crisp paper addressed to her. A distinctly feminine hand met her wary perusal.

The missive was short but incredibly sweet. Jeannette was thrilled to learn she had an older sister and hoped they could meet soon. She apologized for their father's dishonorable behavior and prayed one day Emeline could forgive him. She also hoped Emeline knew she didn't begrudge her the inheritance. The flourishing inscription read:

Your adoring sister,
Jeannette

It was difficult to believe the sincerity of the letter given the rotten nature of their father and brother, but Jeannette had written of her own accord. If she were as angry and spite-filled as Jean Claude, wouldn't she have ignored Emeline? Perhaps even conspired with their brother?

The afternoon had faded into evening, and cracking an eye open, she glanced at the bedside clock. Almost five hours had passed since she'd last seen Liam.

Surely if everything were all right, he would've returned by now. So would have the others.

Fighting tears, she sat up and returned all of the items to their respective boxes.

She'd ask Liam to lock them in his vault. Except for the

letters. She'd read them later. When she'd recovered from the shock she'd sustained this day. A body could only take so many surprises in a day.

"Emeline!"

Her breath caught, and she went perfectly still.

Liam. Praise God.

"Emeline," Liam boomed again. "Where are ye, lass?"

She jumped from the bed and wrenched open her chamber door. "Liam's callin' me," she said unnecessarily to Camden.

With what surely was approval glinting in his eyes, he wordlessly stepped aside.

Not caring who knew her carefully-guarded secret, she tore down the corridor, gown hiked to her knees. At the landing, she pulled up short. Her hand gripping the balustrade, she was suddenly unsure.

Mayhap he only wanted to ensure she was safe.

Except for the Kennedys, his other friends crowded the entry, speaking in low tones.

Yes, he'd kissed her, caressed her, undressed her with his smoldering gray eyes. But he'd never voiced a single syllable that she meant anything to him.

Lady Penderhaven rushed into the entry, immediately followed by Skye and Kendra. She gave her son a fierce hug. "Dinna ye ever worry me like that again, Liam Kirk Fletcher MacKay. I've nae doubt I have several more gray hairs after today."

"The delay was unavoidable," he said soothingly before kissing her cheek.

She stepped back, eyeing him from head to toe and scrunched her aristocratic nose. "Really, Liam, dear. Shouldna ye do somethin' about yer appearance before ye see Emeline? Ye'll frighten her half to death," his mother admonished.

Dirt and blood smeared his face and coat, which hung open, one sleeve ripped almost completely off at the shoulder. His bare knee poked from a hole in his breeches. Even from where Emeline hovered above them, she couldn't miss the bruises and cuts on his knuckles.

He'd never looked more wonderful.

As if sensing Emeline's presence, he glanced up, seeing her poised to flee on the landing. The distance between them vanished, his eyes entreating her and sparking with emotion.

"Emeline," he whispered, raw and yearning. He extended his left arm wide, vulnerable and inviting, and wholly irresistible.

With a strangled joy-filled cry, she flew down the stairs into his warm, perfect embrace. He grunted as she plowed into him before bracing his arm behind her shoulders and pressing her tight to his chest. Nothing had ever felt so absolutely perfectly right. As if she'd finally come home to rest.

In full view of his mother, sister, cousin, and friends, he lowered his mouth to hers. "*Mo chroi.*"

She closed her eyes, twined her arms around his neck, stood on her toes, and kissed him with everything in her heart. *I love ye. I love ye. I love ye.*

"I suppose this means we have a weddin' to plan," Kendra whispered *sotto voce.*

"Jealous?" Broden taunted.

"Do be quiet, ye oaf. Yer interruptin' a romantic moment," Kendra admonished.

Blushing profusely, Emeline settled back on her heels.

"Indeed," came Lady Penderhaven's amused voice. Her

breath caught and she gasped, "Liam?" Panic made her voice strident. "Are ye bleedin'?"

Alarm, icy and shrill, speared Emeline. "Liam?" She retreated a pace, glancing at her blood-dampened gown, then spearing a frantic glance to his side. She pulled the coat away and gasped. "Och, God. There's so much blood."

"'Tis...no...thin', *jo*," he whispered brokenly before his eyes rolled back in his head and his knees buckled.

THIRTEEN

Through oppressive, unyielding layers of fog, wool, and draft horses' wide arses sitting on his eyes, Liam struggled awake. Damn, but his limbs felt leaden, his tongue huge and swollen, and his mouth was as dry as soot and tasted as if swine had mucked about inside.

So damned weak.

He couldn't even lift his arm.

The last thing he remembered was kissing Emeline in front of everyone before everything went black.

"Wh—" A harsh croak emerged from his raw throat.

What he wouldn't give for a drink of cold water. Husbanding the strength to pry his eyelids open, he peered out through the weighty slits. Sticky with sweat, he lay in his bed, a lamp burning low on the mantel. A banked fire glowed in the hearth, and something godawfully heavy held his legs immobile.

Prince?

As if sensing his master had awoken, the dog lifted his head and thumped his tail.

With supreme effort, Liam swallowed and tried to speak again. "What the hell happened?" he said to himself. Eyes gritty and throat shredded as if he'd gargled glass, he'd never felt so wretched in his life. He almost gave up and sank back into blessed oblivion.

Och, Gagneux stabbed me. That sod would threaten Emeline no more. Liam had seen to that.

"Holy hell," he hissed, as searing pain radiated across his torso when he tried to sit up.

He closed his eyes until the wave of agony passed. Tentatively, he brushed his fingertips across the bandages encircling his ribs. Coming in contact with the wound, he winced, cursing the Frenchman to the seventh layer of hell.

The merest noise to his right made him turn his head.

His breath lodged in his throat at the wondrous sight. Fast asleep and fully dressed except for her shoes, Emeline lay curled on her side facing him, one hand tucked beneath her cheek, the other resting on his arm. Her rich bronze hair fanned across the pillow, and, her breathing deep and steady, she slept the slumber of the exhausted.

Because she'd been caring for him?

He rather liked the idea. Liked it a great deal, in fact. He thought his heart might burst, so full of love was he.

In sickness and in health...

Liam took in the soft hand curved around his upper arm, as if, even in sleep, she'd need the physical contact. How could he have not felt her hand the instant he awoke?

A frown drew his brows together.

What in God's holy name was she doing in his bedchamber? If discovered, there'd be no escaping the scandal, even if he had every intention of asking her to become his wife.

"Emeline?"

Her sooty eyelashes fluttered before ever-so-slowly inching upward. Her sleep-clouded, dark honey-colored eyes cleared instantly, and she surged upward, worry and fear washing over her features. At once, she pressed her hand to his forehead, closing her eyes for a blink.

"Och, thank God. Yer fever has broken at last."

Such relief weighted her raspy words, he had cause to wonder how long he'd been ill.

He caught her delicate hand in his. "What happened? How long have I been abed? What time is it?"

"Shh, dinna tire yerself." She placed a finger on his lips, and he kissed the tip. She blushed prettily. "'Tis early evenin'."

"What day?"

Hesitating for an instant, she replied, "Thursday."

"So I've only been unaware for one day?" he asked.

"Nae, Liam." Emeline shook her head, her hair billowing around her shoulders. The ribbon must've come loose while she slept. "Ye've been insensate for eight days."

"Eight days," he croaked.

Eight days?

She speared the bedside clock a swift glance, then took in the drawn draperies as she swept her hair over her shoulder, a tremulous smile on her lips. A becoming blush turned her cheeks rosy again. "I dinna mean to fall asleep. Are ye hungry?"

Was he? He considered the question for a second. "Aye. Verra. And thirsty too. Will ye join me?"

"Aye." A radiant smile blossomed on her face. "I'll order ye a tray and also let yer mother and sister ken ye are awake."

She made to scoot off the bed.

"Wait." He still held her hand. Dark purplish shadows framed her eyes, and a trace of gauntness sharpened her features. "I want to ken what happened."

"Ye remember bein' stabbed?" she asked softly.

"Aye," he gave a slow nod, all the saliva in his mouth gone. "Could I have a drink of water?"

"Of course. I should've thought of that." In one lithe movement, she slid from the bed. Liam loathed releasing her hand, but he was unbearably thirsty. After filling a glass from a covered pitcher on a side table, she brought it to him.

He greedily drank every drop and sighed as she took the glass. "Much better," he said.

"Would ye like more?" She held up the glass.

"Nae." He patted the mattress beside his hip. "Sit down and tell me all. Why do I feel like I've been keelhauled and spent a month in the Sahara?"

"'Twas a nasty gash in yer side, Liam. Verra deep, and ye lost a great deal of blood. The doctor said ye were lucky no organs were injured. The wound had to be cauterized."

Thank God he was unconscious for that ordeal.

Worry stamped on her refined features, her focus dipped to his bandage. "Ye also caught a fever. Ye fought it over a week." She averted her gaze, her throat working as if she fought tears. Despite feeling as week as a kitten, his heart soared. "We feared ye'd succumb, ye were so verra ill," she whispered, her voice quaking.

"And that would've upset ye?" The words formed of their own volition.

Dewy mouth parted, she sliced him an astonished look. "But of course. How can ye even ask such a thing?" She flexed the edges of her eyes slightly. "Liam MacKay. Are ye fishin' for compliments?" Her doe eyes went all soft at the corners, and the radiance of a woman in love glowed on her face. "Ye must ken how I feel about ye."

He lifted her hand and raised it to his lips, placing a kiss on the long fingers. "A man still likes to hear it from the woman who has captivated his heart."

She went as still as a doe in a hunter's sights. Wonder shone in her eyes. "I have yer heart? Truly?"

"Aye, Em." He tugged her nearer, and she came without resistance. "I gave it to ye that day I saved yer life, only I was too stubborn to recognize the feelin's in me. I let scars from the past blind me to what ye meant to me. What we can be together."

"Oh, Liam," she breathed, her eyes sparkling. "Ye have my heart too."

"Come, lay next to me. I need to explain a few things." He drew her down beside him, careful not to disturb his wound. When the soft curves of her body were tucked into his side, her head resting on his shoulder, he ran his fingers through her hair. "I love yer hair. That very first day when I saw it glintin' gloriously in the sun, it enchanted me."

She arched a fine brow. "I had a madman pointin' a gun at me, and ye noticed my bedraggled hair?"

"Aye. And how brave and bold and magnificent ye were." He pressed a kiss to her forehead, aware he probably didn't smell all that fresh and badly needed to cleanse his teeth and shave. "I want ye to ken why I married Kristin."

She shook her head against his shoulder, but he shushed her with a firm squeeze to her waist.

"I need to, lass."

Searching his face, she gave a half-nod. "All right."

Staring blindly at the fireplace, he cleared his throat. This wasn't as easy as he'd believed it would be. "I met Kristin at a house party." He cut her a sidelong glance, noting the doubt in her expression. "Aye, I used to attend such things."

When he'd been young and foolish and headstrong.

Emeline's lips twitched. "Go on," she encouraged gently.

"Four years older than I, she was a widow and the much cossetted and pampered daughter of a moderately wealthy London merchant. When she turned her attention to me, I was flattered. At one and twenty, full of myself and arrogant as hell, I allowed her to turn my head."

He hesitated to tell her this next part. It made him seem like a callow youth.

He had been.

"And...?" Her gaze remained inviting and encouraging, but a slightly tinny tone colored her voice. This was difficult for her as well.

"Kristin was beautiful, confident of her loveliness, and we soon became lovers." He closed his eyes for a moment, wishing he could as easily shut out the memories. "I ignored all the signs that she was more interested in becomin' Baroness Penderhaven. I dinna think she even realized a feudal baron isna part of the aristocracy. Her parents denied her nothin' and made it clear they'd welcome a match between us despite our vast differences. As enamored of her as I was, I wasna ready to commit to marriage. So she and her crafty mother decided to entrap me. They arranged for me to be caught in a...compromisin' situation with her."

Emeline stiffened, radiating outrage. "That's utterly despicable."

"She also claimed she was with child, so we wed. I stupidly

believed her and believed we could be happy, even though I kent she was spoiled. Even after I discovered she wasna with child as she'd claimed. The first year was tolerable." He rubbed his stubbled chin.

"But...?" she gently prompted.

Liam knew she asked for his sake. So he'd finally be freed from his past, not because she had any craving to know the sordid details.

"But after the bairns came," he said, "she drank more and more and kept threatenin' to take the wee ones and leave. I couldna bear the idea. Although, as a man, I had the legal control of our children, I didna want to deprive her of them. In her way, Kristin loved the bairns, and children need a mother. Even if she isna a very good one." His voice had dropped to a rough whisper, whether from talking so much or from the anguish Kristin's betrayal had wrought, he couldn't say.

"I'm sorry, Liam." Emeline gripped his hand. "She sounds like a tortured soul who thought ye were the answer to her unhappiness and grew increasingly bitter when she realized ye werena."

"Where did ye acquire such wisdom?" He stroked her cheek.

She chuckled. "Ye'd be amazed at what I heard in my aunt's shop, some of which was useful, but mostly tattle that burned my innocent ears."

"I was a gullible idiot, and my foolishness cost my precious bairns their lives." He blinked away the moisture blinding him.

She propped herself on an elbow, her intelligent eyes scouring his face. She traced his scar, then pressed a kiss to the jagged flesh. If he hadn't been as frail as a newborn foal, he'd have taken her right then and there. Made her his for all time.

"What could ye have done differently?" she asked, the question sincere. "She came to yer bed willingly when there was nae understandin' between ye. As a widow, she kent what to expect. When she lied and said she was with child, ye did the honorable thing and married her. And when she grew more and more difficult, ye still tried to be honorable for the sake of yer children."

She made it sound so reasonable, so matter of fact. She readily absolved Liam for the things he'd had no control over. God knew he didn't deserve such forgiveness.

Compassion crimping her eyes, she shook her head. "I canna think ye could've done anythin' differently. Ye werena the problem. She was."

"I also killed yer brother," he said, more abruptly than he'd intended. "I dinna ken how, but he kent we were comin'. He had four men waitin' to ambush us."

"Did ye have any other choice?" The color drained from her face, but she didn't break eye contact.

Drawing his mouth into a grim line, Liam gave one short jerk of his head. "I tried to take him alive, but he was crazed with rage and jealousy. He swore he'd never rest until ye were dead. I am sorry though. He was yer kin, even if ye didna ken him."

"I have a sister too."

Liam angled his head, interest in his eyes. "Ye do? How do ye ken?"

Emeline succinctly told him about the wills, the birth and marriage records, and the letters from her father and sister.

"It seems I'm an heiress." Two lines creasing her brow, her

expression took on a faraway look. "I think I shall have to write to my sister, at the very least. Or perhaps invite her here. I dinna think she has anyone now."

"What if she's like her brother?" Liam didn't like the idea at all. He knew firsthand how conniving women could be. The sister had gone from being a woman of substance and position to an illegitimate progeny with few, if any, prospects unless things were a far cry different in France than England or Scotland.

She shook her head. "I dinna think she is. Her name is Jeannette, and she sent a letter too. In it, she was very gracious."

"Enough talk of negative things." Wincing, he turned slightly onto his side. Gritting his teeth, he opened the bedside table and withdrew the ring box. He removed the ring and dropped the box before turning back to her. "I have the most wonderful woman in the whole of the world in my bed, and I need to ask her somethin' verra important."

He slipped the ring on her finger, delighted the color almost exactly matched her glorious eyes.

Hope vied with doubt in Emeline's expressive gaze as she looked at the ring. Her attention dipped to his lips for a half-second and she said with caution, "But ye said ye'd never marry me."

"I was an unmitigated arse. An absolute inconsiderate, selfish dolt. Please forgive me, *leannan*, I—" Stopping abruptly, he scowled.

"What is it, Liam?"

"Now that ye're an heiress, perchance ye're no' interested in weddin'," he said. "Mayhap, ye want to travel—"

"Hush, ye silly man." Emeline rolled closer, placing her

left hand on his chest over his heart. "There's nothin' on this earth I'd rather do than marry ye."

"Are ye absolutely certain?" She must be. He'd not marry her if she had a single doubt.

She raised her head to plant a kiss on his mouth. "Aye, my Highland warrior." A deliciously naughty gleam entered her eyes as she slid her hands over his shoulders. "Aye. Let me show ye how much."

EPILOGUE

Eytone Hall, Scottish Highlands
December 1721

A palm pressed against the icy window pane, Emeline stood enthralled as great fat snowflakes sifted from the sooty sky. She'd seen snow before, of course, but never in this quantity. It had begun yesterday morning and hadn't stopped. A thick, virginal mantle blanketed the entire Highlands. Beautiful and peaceful.

A private smile curved her mouth as contentment she couldn't have imagined flowed through her like warmed honey.

If the weather permitted, Liam had promised to take her sleighing on the morrow. Their houseguests were as enthusiastic about the outing as she. Jeannette, now living at Eytone Hall and Liam's ward, had proved to be the sister Emeline had always wanted.

They even looked much like one another, except

Jeannette's hazel eyes simmered with a hint of mischief Emeline's never had. As sweet and sincere as their brother had been evil and calculating, Jeannette had adjusted surprisingly well to her change in circumstances and to living in the Highlands.

Emeline had the privilege of meeting Pierre Durpreiz when he'd escorted Jeannette to her new home. He'd been as charming and kind as Aunt Jeneva had vowed him to be. He wrote her regularly now and had almost convinced her to journey to France to view her estates once the plague had been eradicated.

Quinn and Skye were houseguests too.

Last year, Skye had introduced a few of her favorite Yuletide traditions. Recovering from the sudden deaths of both parents within a week of each other in October of 1720, she'd thrown herself into the holiday preparations as a way of honoring them as well as needing the distraction to help deal with her grief.

The result of her efforts had been a season so memorable that, although Scots didn't celebrate the holiday in the same fashion as the English, Liam and Emeline had decided that, at Eytone Hall, Christmastide would be observed in the more traditional, festive way.

Kendra and Broden had arrived two days ago, as had Berget and Graeme and a few others. Arieen's time drew near, so she wasn't able to come. However, she'd vowed to be the first to arrive next year. Logan and Mayra Rutherford had sent their apologies as well, wanting to remain near Arieen, as well as having a reluctance to travel with their two-month-old daughter, especially after Mayra had miscarried last year.

The house overflowed with family, friends, and love.

"Lass, come to bed," Liam murmured from the comfort of the large curtained bed dominating the room. "I dinna want yer frozen toes and bum assailin' me again," he teased.

Turning from the window, Emeline tilted her head coyly, all but purring, "I dinna hear ye complainin' about my bum this mornin' when ye—"

"Woman. Bed. Now." A mocking smile quirked his well-formed mouth.

"Och, I dinna think so." Emeline made a pretense of sauntering to the fireplace, swinging her hips provocatively. Liam particularly adored her bum. Gathering the curtain of her hair, she bent over and poked the fire, aware she gave her husband of just over a year a view he very much admired.

Before she straightened, strong arms encircled her from behind. "Ye promised to *obey* me, serve me, love, honor, and keep me," he whispered in her ear, his tone husky with unappeased desire.

"I think that was more of a suggestion rather than an absolute decree." She turned in his embrace. "Besides, ye, Liam MacKay, Baron Penderhaven, like the chase. Admit it. As long as ye ken the outcome." She bent her neck and placed a hot, opened-mouthed kiss on his pectoral muscles.

The sculpted flesh—pure masculine rawness—jumped beneath her lips, and she smiled against his fragrant skin. Had any man ever smelled so...masculine? She loved that she could make him respond like this. A mere look or an innocent touch and Liam became a blazing conflagration. And when he took her to his bed, *God above*, no woman had ever experienced such bone-melting ecstasy.

He lowered her to the fur before the roaring hearth, the hard angles of his beloved face standing out harshly with his passion. "Emeline MacKay, I love ye," he murmured into the sensitive hollow where her neck met her collarbone.

He'd learned all of her most sensitive places and didn't hesitate to exploit his knowledge to his advantage. Not that she minded overly much.

Arching her neck to allow him greater access, she trailed her fingertips over the ridges and swells she knew as well as her own body. Perhaps better. "And I ye, Liam, master of my heart."

He moved to her mouth, his tongue dueling with hers as his manhood nudged insistently at the apex of her thighs. Would she ever tire of this joining? Of becoming one with this man who touched so much more than her physical body but who'd taken her heart captive? He'd stamped his spirit upon hers for all time.

"Look at me, Em," Liam insisted, his head poised at her entrance.

She couldn't deny him. Lifting her gaze to his, she read the adoration there and knew he could see the same in her eyes.

A soft moan escaped from her parted lips as he slid into her, and soon they were swept into the current of blissful sensation, their hearts and souls melding as one.

"Liam!" Emeline cried as the first powerful tremors sluiced through her, spiraling her higher and higher until everything exploded into wave after wave of exquisite pleasure.

His release came on the heels of hers and, with a guttural groan and a final hard thrust, he spent himself. Liam rolled onto his back, taking her with him. Eyes closed, he trailed his fingers in large figure eights across her back and buttocks.

"Liam?"

"Hmm," came his relaxed, satiated, and nearly inaudible reply.

"I have a surprise for ye."

One quicksilver eye cracked open. "A good surprise or one I'd rather no' hear until mornin'?" He screwed his mouth to the side. "Dinna tell me Arieen had her bairn? Is it a wee lass or laddie?" Positive he'd discovered her secret, he beamed, cocksure and proud.

She chuckled, running her fingers through his chest hair. "Nae, no' yet, though verra soon. 'Tis about a bairn. Berget and Skye are with child too. They told me yesterday. Both are due the beginnin' of summer."

Despite the hearty blaze a few feet from them, now that her ardor had cooled, her flesh prickled with cold. Even so, she was loath to leave her husband's arms. Here, the world's cares and worries fell away. In his embrace, time stood still, and only this wondrous unity mattered. Why, their breathing had even taken on the same rhythm.

"'Tis what happens when a man and woman love each other," he said softly, almost reverently. "A child born of such a union is the ultimate gift, a culmination of love, and the bairn is blessed from its verra conception."

Her eyes pooled with tears at the loveliness of his words as much as the melancholic note that had seeped into his melodious baritone. He so longed for another child, and each month when her flow came and she disappointed him, she wanted to weep.

Emeline didn't doubt he thought of Joseph and Mareona. She visited their graves weekly, sometimes taking flowers, often wondering who they would have become had they lived.

Those first few months, Liam couldn't bear to go with her, but time had begun to heal that wound too. He'd always carry the scar of their deaths—how could he not?—but inch by determined inch, he'd been able to move forward with his life.

And isn't that what mattered?

Persevering in the face of impossible adversity? Clinging to hope that tomorrow would be better in some small way than today?

One leg slung over his hairy thigh, she drew little circles on his chest. The long, freshly pink scar marring his torso still made her cringe. She'd come so petrifyingly close to losing him. She buried her nose in his shoulder and hugged him fiercely.

Kissing the top of her head, he asked, "What's this surprise?"

"Ye'll have to wait until July to find out."

"July?" came his puzzled reply. Then he went utterly still. Except for the snapping fire and ticking clock, silence enshrouded the bedchamber.

At last, unable to bear the strain any longer, she lifted her head, meeting his flummoxed eyes. Suspicious moisture glinted at the corners along with desperate hope and a shred of fear too.

"*Jo*, do ye mean...?"

Unable to contain her joy for an instant longer, she braced herself on his chest. Smiling, she nodded. "'Tis what happens when a man and woman love each other."

If you'd like to leave a review, please scan the QR code.

Keep reading for a free preview of
TO ENCHANT A HIGHLAND EARL
Heart of a Scot Series, Book Five

Scottish Highlands
Mid-January 1721

Clenching the wadded letter tightly in his fist, Broden pivoted on his heels and tramped the reverse path across the smooth flagstone floor. His boot heels rapped dully off the book-laden shelves and the dark paneled walls of the masculine chamber acting as his library, private sitting room, and study.

His heartbeat whooshed in his ears, a peculiarly muffled tempo, like someone striking a drum covered by a thick pile of blankets.

The fire in the hearth sizzled as occasional droplets of rain survived the treacherous descent down the chimney only to splutter to a quick death. Outside, a deluge poured from the contemptuous pewter-gray clouds as the biting winter wind assailed everything in its path with unrelenting resolve to pummel and saturate.

He supposed he ought to be grateful it wasn't snowing.

A particularly powerful gust buffeted the sturdy

rectangular stone house, causing the windowpanes to rattle and the unremarkable man sitting at Broden's desk to cast a wary glance out the rain-splattered glass.

No doubt, Mr. Philibius Oswald, Solicitor, worried about his return journey to Eddleshaugh.

As well he should.

If the weather remained this dismal—a savvy chap would wager on it—Oswald would be obliged to take a room at one of Eddleshaugh's inns. After he and the sorry nag he'd arrived upon had slogged the almost two miles to the township. At this juncture, the much-traveled tracks to Edinburgh and then London would be impassable if the torrent kept up. Given the ashen sky, that seemed certain.

After all, this was January in the Highlands. One could expect rain and snow. Snow and rain. Then more of the same.

Every bit as certain as the intractable weather's continuation was another simple fact: Broden wouldn't extend his hospitality and offer the attorney a bed for the night. Or two or three if the tempest lingered. Not after learning why Oswald had stupidly—*Sassenach idiot*—braved the storm and called unannounced.

An entirely different sort of storm brewed within the cozy study, though no less fierce or ruthless in its fury. As Broden struggled to accept the life-altering news he'd just received—*Goddammit to hell*—anger and disbelief vied for supremacy in every pore. Pores humming and pulsating and expanding in a silent but raucous chorus of strain and vexation.

And the news... A groan of despair almost escaped past his meshed lips. News he'd never conceived nor expected to hear; not in a hundred—no, a thousand—lifetimes.

God's hairy ballocks, he swore irreverently to himself.

Surely, it was a gargantuan mistake. An enormous, colossal error. A careless clerical blunder or a misprint on some long-ago faded, forgotten, and moldy kirk registry. Someone, somewhere *had* to have made a mistake.

He could not be—most assuredly did not *want* to be—the next Earl of Montforth. Plowing his free hand through his hair, he dislodged the ribbon that kept it tied in a queue at his nape. Earl or not, he wasn't donning a ridiculous curling wig or powdering his hair for anyone.

He was not a mincing fop.

"There's nae one else to inherit?" he demanded of the solicitor, aware but beyond caring that the man simply performed his duties.

Dinna kill the messenger and all that twaddin' shite.

The silent reminder to himself did nothing to lessen his ire. His helplessness. The acerbic frustration. The unequivocal feeling of being trapped. Ensnared. *Imprisoned.*

He jabbed a finger toward the man of law, idly noting the dirt packed beneath the man's nails. Earls didn't have dirty fingernails. Or hands. Neither did they muck out stalls, move rocks from grazing, and farm the land. Or chop their own firewood.

"Ye're absolutely—without a *single* doubt—positive ye havena made a mistake?" he asked.

Oswald vacillated for a long blink, his Adam's apple rapidly cresting and sinking like a miniature boat caught upon the tidal surges of a massive, violent storm. And his tiny ship was about to flounder.

"There *is* another distant *English* cousin," the fusty attorney reluctantly confessed. His eyebrows—wiry copperish things with minds of their own and an unfortunate proclivity to wriggle about on his forehead—huddled together over the pronounced bridge of his beaked nose.

"Aye? *And*?" Broden encouraged, grasping at even the weakest straw. Anything to keep him from plummeting into the loony world of the aristocracy.

"In truth, he's already contacted me in anticipation—" Oswald faltered, realizing he'd disclosed confidential information. His nervous gaze bounced about the room, landing everywhere but on Broden.

So, the other chap thought to inherit.

Interesting.

Convenient?

Could such a blessed thing be arranged?

Suddenly finding the well-thumbed documents before him of acute interest, Mr. Philibius Oswald cleared his throat. "But you, my lord, are indisputably the *next* in line. I informed him as much, unequivocally. You needn't fear he'll supersede you."

"How did he take it?"

"I beg your pardon?" From the solicitor's gaping jaw and buggy eyes, Broden might have asked him when he'd last swived.

"Was he upset?" He was in no temper to dance around the point or use flowery phrases.

"Naturally, he was—ah—somewhat nonplussed." Oswald chose his words with obvious care. "But I believe he understands the rules governing ennoblement, the letters patent, and the specifics of the remainder are beyond our control. Which is to say, he cannot inherit as long as you are alive."

Och, well, there went that idea all to piss.

Broden didn't miss the pinched expression tightening

Oswald's thin face as he admitted that fact. The Englishman assuredly would've preferred his countryman inherit the title, rather than an uncouth, lowborn Scot of questionable comportment and an even more questionable liking for the English.

"His name?" he asked, tempering his impatience.

But only just.

"Mr. Edwin Archibald Wiggins McGregor."

Pompous. Traditional. Unimaginative. A worthy Sassenach name, except for the family surname, that was. McGregor, after all, was a derivative of the Gaelic MacGriogair. Scots through and through, no matter how much Oswald would prefer it otherwise.

"*He* attended Oxford," Oswald added with the merest haughty sniff.

La de dah.

"He's well-traveled and already acquainted with several members of the peerage," the attorney droned on as if listing Edwin's stellar attributes ought to impress Broden.

Or did Oswald prattle on to jab a particular point home?

To demonstrate how much more Edwin was qualified for the title?

As Broden didn't give a hog's teat about Edwin Archibald Wiggins McGregor, not even to pity the man his unfortunate third name, Oswald's intentions missed their mark.

"Ye dinna say?" Each word dripping with sarcasm, he schooled his features into a false expression of suitable admiration. "He sounds like a paragon of society."

Och, I've been to England and France, and I count a half dozen Scots lairds as my friends. I dinna suppose the skinny turd cares about that, though.

"Mr. Archibald McGregor is an investor." If Oswald lifted his nose any higher in self-importance, he might well drown when he left the house.

If that meant Broden might be free of the mammoth burden just dumped upon him, he could be persuaded to look the other way and permit the man to suffer the consequence of his arrogance.

That thought brought him reluctantly 'round to the matter at hand once more.

He was an earl. And, by Odin's toes, he very much didn't want to be.

Mouth cinched into a grim, unyielding line, he leveled the solicitor a steely stare.

"Pray tell me, Mr. Oswald, why I am just now learnin' of my change in circumstances via this?" Broden jerked his hand up, uncurling his fingers around the mashed missive with its dangling black ribbon and seal-imprinted crimson wax. "My predecessor died over a year ago."

Oswald, a gangly fellow, all lanky arms and legs and spindly fingers flicked a disinterested look at the balled paper before bringing his keen, hazel gaze up to scrutinize Broden's features. He examined him for an extended moment, taking in his soiled and mended work clothing, scuffed boots, unkempt and unbound hair, and beard-stubbled face as if searching for something.

For what?

"You do bear a vague resemblance to the late earl." He wiggled his twiggy fingers near his angular face. "In the angles and bone structure of your chin and jaw, though your physique is much more...ah..." He lowered his assessing gaze to take in Broden's shoulders and chest. "*Robust.*"

Meaning, his dead kin had most likely been a milksop and a prancing, affected popinjay.

Had he worn stays?

Broden had heard some Englishmen padded their clothing to enhance certain anatomical features and also wore stays to diminish others.

Broden used the occasion to take the solicitor's measure too.

At odds with his fastidious behavior, gravy stains marred Oswald's buff-toned, wrinkled waistcoat and a shock of fuzzy red-brown hair poked straight up from atop his otherwise bald pate. Almost as if someone had forgotten to shave the rest of the unfortunate man's pointed head.

It rather gave the man the appearance of a paintbrush.

He peered over the round wire-rims of his spectacles. Seemingly unaffected by either Broden's superior size or his obvious vexation, he calmly lifted the corner of another document he'd pulled from his brown leather portfolio.

"Mr. McGregor—?" The lawyer flushed blotchy red. "I beg your pardon."

He noisily cleared his throat and began again.

"*My lord*, the prior earl was most emphatic that in the event of his death, his heir only be notified when it became abundantly clear that the title would not pass to a progeny of his loins. As his wife was with child at the time of his lordship's unfortunate death, prudence demanded postponing the pronouncement of the fifth Earl of Montforth until the babe's birth seven months later."

A bloody Sassenach earl.

How in all of Christendom had such a wholly preposterous thing occurred?

The earldom did lay just inside the British side of the borderlands, but still...

His focus beyond the soggy landscape visible through the windows, Broden scrunched his eyes and rubbed his chin. Wasn't there something he'd heard once about a long-ago relative scampering off with a noble decades before?

Was that the connection?

His mother might recall.

He'd have to ask her after Oswald took his leave.

As the attorney had explained, somewhere in the gnarly, extended, and complex family tree, Broden and the previous earl had shared ancestral blood.

Where, precisely, was unclear to him.

"I take it the bairn was a wee lass?" Working his thumb across the stiff wax seal, Broden regarded the attorney. There was something about the man that raised his hackles. Something besides him being an Englishman and a slimy solicitor to boot.

In short, he didn't trust the man.

Perhaps a visit to Oswald's London offices was in order.

Oswald sighed as he removed his spectacles and wiped the lenses with a less than pristine handkerchief he'd lifted from his inside coat pocket. "Seven children in nine years and the only surviving offspring are all daughters. Five, to be precise."

Standish had been a busy man, and mayhap not a complete peacock if he sired that many bairns. Or perhaps, he'd just been desperate to beget an heir. A sliver of pity for Standish's wife poked Broden.

"And quite naturally, it did take several months to locate the next male in line for the title," Oswald blathered on. "We exhausted all of our leads in England before resorting to directing our attention to Scotland."

As he tapped a bony finger atop the scarred and scuffed desk, the man's contempt was fairly palpable. He seemed no keener to tell Broden of his new title than he was to learn of the bloody nuisance.

He heartily wished he *hadn't* been found.

"The law is *very* clear, my lord. You...," he glanced down at the page before him, his brow knitted. "Broden Lachlan Errol McGregor, *are* the fifth Earl of Montforth."

Oswald's nasally, clipped tones set Broden's teeth on edge. Not good, considering a very fine tether held his ire in check.

The fire popped and snapped as a log fell, disintegrating into glowing, crimson-orange coals. More for a need to do something than to build the flames once more, Broden laid the letter atop the mantel beside a bronze candlestick, then knelt and added another log to the blaze. With the poker, he shoved a few coals beneath the new addition, coaxing the fire, and soon hungry flames licked up the sides.

He set the poker in place before planting his palms on his thighs and pushing upright once more, accompanied by a hefty, resigned sigh.

Christ and all the angels would descend from heaven before he trotted himself off to England to claim a Sassenach earldom. *God's teeth.* He could already hear Liam MacKay's and Graeme Kennedy's mocking chortles. Logan Rutherford and Coburn Wallace would be utterly unbearable.

"What if I refuse?"

"*Refuse?* Why... Why... You cannot." Rapidly blinking his eyes owl-like behind his lenses, Oswald spluttered like a stubby candle's flame about to die. "The title *is* yours. *Yours.*"

Yes, definite scorn riddled his terse speech.

"What *you* do with the honor is, of course, up to you. But there is no question of not accepting," the solicitor insisted. "You are the Earl of Montforth until you depart this earth, my lord."

Just because the paperwork *said* he was an earl didn't mean Broden must adjust his life one iota. He leaned a shoulder against the stone mantel—stones which had been cleared from his lands by his two-times-two grandfather—and crossed his arms. "And if I choose to ignore it and continue as I have for the past three decades?"

Oswald raised his bland gaze for a moment before attending to his spectacles once more. Something deep within the depths of his eyes shifted. The briefest flash before he sank his attention to cleaning his eyewear.

"As you can imagine, my lord, Lady Montforth is quite beside herself, awaiting news of her future and that of her children. She is a gentle creature, devoted to her daughters, and the epitome of refinement."

Aye, Broden grudgingly admitted to himself. The countess was in a precarious predicament through no fault of her own.

"The household staff, the tenants, not to mention the villagers, all await your directives." Oswald spoke clearly and deliberately as if striving to make a bacon brain or mutton head understand a complex mathematical formula. "These past months have been a hardship for them all as the stewards and solicitors could only make superficial decisions."

The twig of a man all but implied Broden owed it to those people he'd never met—strangers—to ensure their futures and well-being. He wasn't a selfish man, by God, but to uproot himself and charge off to England? To become part of that uppity set—the haughty aristocrats who looked down their snooty noises upon the Scots?

Nae.

Not as long as he drew a breath.

The familial home he shared with his mother, a cook, a maid of all work, and, on occasion, his childhood friend, Quinn Catherwood, until he'd married last Christmastide, was simple but comfortable.

And the eighteen acres he owned, which fed sheep, a few cows, and other livestock quite nicely. Conveniently, a brook rambled through the northernmost edge of his property, where he enjoyed fishing as time permitted.

He also employed two laborers who tended everything from the garden to the stables, and he worked alongside them at whatever task most needed completing. Hence his dirty nails and soiled garments today.

Broden highly doubted the previous Earls of Montforth had ever even broken a sweat, let alone cleaned hog sties, dug peat, helped deliver lambs, or used a blade upon another man.

Though he'd never attended a fancy university, Broden was well-educated and knew how to wield a sword and a dirk, thanks to his scholarly father's tutelage. And thanks to his mother, he could maneuver a ballroom when required to dance and spoke a dab of French. When pressed, he could conduct himself like the poshest of gentlemen.

But don the shroud of a noble?

An earl?

Wouldn't that make him the worst sort of hypocrite?

"At the very least, I would expect, your lordship, that you'd *want* to examine your holdings." Oswald rubbed his reedy nose, leaving a faint ink trail down the side. "After all,

Sommerley Parke House is not even two days' journey from here."

A better man might've told the man of law about the ink smear.

Broden wasn't such a man.

With the smudge on his thin nose, Oswald resembled an over-sized rodent. Appropriate, since Broden regarded all attorneys as vermin. He had yet to meet one who didn't serve his selfish interests first. Oh, no doubt there were a good number of ethical and honest lawyers in their field. He'd just not had the privilege of meeting one as yet.

"I suppose you could hire a man of business to oversee your estate or expand the duties of your current stewards," Oswald continued, as if thinking aloud, his eyes slightly narrowed and fingers loosely steepled. "The countess did ask me to inquire what your wishes are for her and her daughters—now your wards. Should they remain at Sommerley Parke House? Retire to the dower house? One of the other estates? Bellewaite House? Come here?"

Dower house? Other estates?

Wait, the bloody hell!

Here? Them come here?

Where in God's name would he put six females and no doubt a lady's maid for the countess, a nanny for the youngest girls, a governess for the older lasses, and a nurse for the infant?

"Shite," Broden swore beneath his breath, furious and foul.

The care of the former earl's wife and five daughters were now his responsibility. *Hell and damnation.* He'd never even met Standish, the fourth earl, and certainly never anticipated inheriting.

Inheriting?

Derision curled his lip.

He hadn't even been aware of the title until Oswald, very much appearing like a drowning mongrel, had banged most insistently upon his door two hours ago.

Broden's mother coughed delicately before entering with a laden tray. Her lace cap flapped upon her graying hair as she limped to the low table before a well-worn, sage-green sofa.

Damp weather always made her joints stiffen and ache. Rather than waiting upon him and Oswald, she ought to be snuggled in her bed sipping a hot willow bark and turmeric toddy, heated flannel encasing her legs, and a ripping good book between her work-worn hands.

"Mr. Oswald," she said with a cheery smile, "I'm certain ye must be famished."

Her simple plaid gown and white apron pinned to the front bespoke a woman of gentle but humble means. The McGregors weren't impoverished by any stretch, but neither were they affluent.

Oswald perked up as the aromas of Scotch pies and warm bread wafted from the tray's direction.

"Indeed, Mrs. McGregor. A most welcome respite." Oswald stacked his papers into a neat pile. Once he'd closed the inkpot, he hurried to the sofa and availed himself of a Scotch pie.

Mother poured him a cup of coffee. "Broden, would ye care for coffee?"

"Nae." He strode to his desk and pulled open the bottom drawer. Removing a glass and a whisky bottle, he poured three finger's worth of the dark, amber liquid. Reluctantly, he angled the bottle toward Oswald. "Whisky, Oswald?"

The solicitor lifted his long nose, his nostrils flaring in distaste. "Thank you, no. I've found Scottish spirits are too strong for my palate."

Och, the toff probably takes milk in his coffee too.

Before Broden had finished the thought, Oswald said, "May I impose upon you to add milk to my coffee and three sugar lumps, Mrs. McGregor?"

"Aye." His mother swiftly complied, her right eyebrow elevated. That always meant she had a great deal more to say but had elected to hold her sharp tongue, which could strip a heather bush bare when she was incensed.

Broden, on the other hand, had to bite his tongue to keep from telling the rickle-a-bones his mother wasn't a servant.

A fine line pulling her eyebrows together, his mother peered at him with knowing, pale brown eyes. Eyes very much like his own. The hue not quite the shade of strong tea but more fawn colored. "Are ye no' eatin', Son?"

"I shall later." He dropped a kiss onto the crown of her head as he wrapped an arm around her shoulder. "Why dinna ye rest now? I ken this damp weather wreaks havoc on yer joints."

Her gaze avid with curiosity, she sent the solicitor a considering look.

A wry, mocking smile skewed Broden's mouth at her not-so-subtle hint. "I'll tell ye everythin'—"

"The earldom owns houses in Brighton and London as well," Oswald said between bites and uncouth, appreciative noises. "One of those climes might be beneficial to your health, Mrs. McGregor."

In England?

Not bloody likely.

Broden lanced the man through with his gaze. Did he truly think to manipulate him by playing upon his sympathies?

"Earldom?" His mother's attention swept between the men. "Have ye inherited Standish's title, Broden?"

She knew about the title?

I hope you enjoyed this free preview of
TO ENCHANT A HIGHLAND EARL
Heart of a Scot
Book Five

My research for this story proved quite fascinating. As I explored flash floods in Scotland, I discovered that even as I wrote this tale, several flash floods had impacted Scotland in 2019, including one in Edinburgh.

The Great Plague of Marseille, for which I based the plague in France in my story, began in 1720 and lasted until 1722, killing over 100,000 people. Though I didn't mention the cause of Emeline's father's death, I left it to the reader to surmise how he died. I also hinted why Skye's father was so ill. This outbreak was the last major epidemic of bubonic plague in Europe.

I would be remiss if I didn't mention the Christmastide gathering Liam and Emeline host at Eytone Hall. An Act of Parliament in 1640 labeled "Yule vacation" celebrations paganistic and illegal in Scotland. Oliver Cromwell also banned Christmas. Up until that time, the Christmastide had been a religious festival celebrated in much the same way the holiday was kept in Catholic Europe with feasts, gifts, games, and of course, church services.

The act prohibiting Christmas was repealed in 1686, but Christmas wasn't *officially* celebrated as a public holiday by the Scots again until 1958. However, according to my research, many Scots privately celebrated a subdued variation of the religious holiday, but not Yule. Those who did so were subject to fines and even imprisonment. I've taken literary license to include a celebration for my Heart of a Scot characters, introduced by an English character who adores the holiday.

To make sure you don't miss news about my books, subscribe to my newsletter (Get a free book too!). I also have a fabulous VIP Reader Group on Facebook Collette's Chéris. If you're a fan of my books and historical romance, I'd love to have you join me. You'll also be the first to see new covers, read exclusive excerpts, be the first to know about contests and give-aways, help me pick titles and name characters, and much, much more!

I had so much fun researching and writing TO WOO A HIGHLAND WARRIOR, and I hope you enjoyed reading Liam and Emeline's story. If so, be sure to check out the other books in my HEART OF A SCOT SERIES. Please consider telling other readers why you enjoyed this book by reviewing it as well. I also truly adore hearing from my readers. You can contact me on my website, info@collettecameronbooks.com and while you are there, explore my author world.

Hugs,
Collette

If you haven't joined Collette's exclusive mailing list click on QR image to sign up! You'll get access to exclusive content, sneak peeks, contests, giveaways, and more...

(P.S. No spam!)

https://collettecameronbooks.com/freegift

Collette loves to hear from readers.
You can contact her via her website: collettecameron-books.com.
Or email her directly at collette@collettecameron-books.com.

You can also follow Collette on social media:
Facebook: https://www.facebook.com/ColletteCameronNovels/
Instagram: https://instagram.com/collettecameronauthor/
Goodreads: https://www.goodreads.com/collettecameron

Book Bub: https://www.bookbub.com/authors/collette-cameron
Pinterest: http://www.pinterest.com/colletteauthor/
YouTube: https://www.youtube.com/@ColletteCameronAuthor

Giggles are Guaranteed
Collette's Cheris Reader Group

https://www.facebook.com/groups/CollettesCheris/

If you love to chat about all things romance-book related and enjoy taking part in fun and engaging live events, contests, and giveaways join **Collette's Chèris VIP Reader Group, https://www.facebook.com/groups/CollettesCheris/,** my exclusive private book group on Facebook.

Giggles are guaranteed!

Hope to see you there,
Collette Cameron®

ABOUT THE AUTHOR

COLLETTE CAMERON®

USA Today Bestselling author Collette Cameron® is renowned for her captivating, humorous, and heartwarming Scottish and Regency historical romance novels. With over 65 published titles, over 1.6 million books sold around the world, and multiple writing awards to her credit, Collette is a well-known author in the world of historical romance.

Readers love her witty and relatable characters including daring rogues, dashing scoundrels, and the strong and spirited heroines who capture their hearts. From the rugged highlands to the refined drawing rooms of Regency England, Collette's novels will transport you to another time and place, where love and adventure are just a page away.

Collette's Sweet-to-Spicy Timeless Romances® are the perfect escape for readers looking for romantic escape, poignant inspiration, engaging humor, and entertaining stories.

Based in the Pacific Northwest, Collette is surrounded by the lush greenery and rainy skies that inspire her writing. She dreams of one day splitting her time between the Pacific Northwest and Scotland. In the meantime, she indulges in her love of all things cobalt blue, dachshunds, chocolate, and of course, crafting her next historical romance.

Blue Rose Romance® LLC
collette@collettecameronbooks.com
collettecameronbooks.com

FOR THE LOVE OF AN EARL (Wicked Earls' Club)

A Humorous Aristocrat and Wallflower

Regency Romance Adventure

HEART OF A SCOT

THE CULPEPPER MISSES

A Humorous Wallflower Family Saga

Regency Romantic Comedy

The Earl and the Spinster — Book 1

The Marquis and the Vixen — Book 2

The Lord and the Wallflower — Book 3

The Buccaneer and the Bluestocking — Book 4

The Lieutenant and the Lady — Book 5

THE HONORABLE ROGUES®

A Second Chance Redeemable Rogue

and Wallflower Regency Romance

A Kiss for a Rogue — Book 1

A Bride for a Rogue — Book 2

A Rogue's Scandalous Wish — Book 3

To Capture a Rogue's Heart — Book 4

The Rogue and the Wallflower — Book 5

A Rose for a Rogue — Book 6

'Twas the Rogue Before Christmas — Book 7

A Rogue Worth the Risk — Book 8